Tuesdays with Matthew

an apostle,

a photographer,

and life's greatest questions

by

Mike Nappa

RIVEROAK®
PUBLISHING

River Oak® is an imprint of
Cook Communications Ministries, Colorado Springs, CO 80918
Cook Communications, Paris, Ontario
Kingsway Communications, Eastbourne, England

TUESDAYS WITH MATTHEW
© 2003 by Nappaland Communications Inc.

All rights reserved. No part of this book may be reproduced without written permission, except for brief quotations in books and critical reviews. For information, write Cook Communications Ministries, 4050 Lee Vance View, Colorado Springs, CO 80918.

First printing, 2003
Printed in the United States of America

1 2 3 4 5 6 7 8 9 10 Printing/Year 07 06 05 04 03

Editor: Craig Bubeck, Sr. Editor
Cover & Interior Design: YaYe Design

TUESDAYS WITH MATTHEW is published in association with the literary agency of Nappaland Communications Inc. To contact a Nappaland author, access the free webzine for families at: www.Nappaland.com.
This book is a work of fiction. Names, characters, places, and incidents are either products of the author's imagination or used fictitiously. Any similarity to actual people, organizations, and/or events is purely coincidental.

Portions of dialogue attributed to the character of Matthew in this book are quoted from the gospel of Matthew in the Bible. Unless otherwise noted, Scripture quotations are taken from the *Holy Bible: New International Version®*. Copyright © 1973, 1978, 1984 by International Bible Society. Used by permission of Zondervan Publishing House. All rights reserved.

Scripture quotations marked (NLT) are taken from the *Holy Bible, New Living Translation*, copyright © 1996. Used by permission of Tyndale House Publishers, Inc., Wheaton, IL 60189. All rights reserved.

Library of Congress Cataloging-in-Publication Data

Nappa, Mike, 1963-
  Tuesdays with Matthew : an apostle, a photographer, and life's greatest questions / by Mike Nappa.
      p. cm.
Includes bibliographical references.
  ISBN 0-7814-3871-3 (pbk.)
  1. Matthew, the Apostle, Saint--Fiction. 2. Conduct of life--Fiction.
3. Photographers--Fiction. 4. Apostles--Fiction. I. Title.
  PS3564.A624 T84 2003
  813'.54--dc21

For Amy! (As usual.)

M.N.

"Come, be my disciple."
—Jesus Christ, to a tax collector, long ago[1]

Contents

Prologue

HE WAS SHORTER than I expected. I mean, at only 5 foot 9 inches myself, I'm no Goliath. Most guys I meet are 6 feet tall or higher, and I'm used to doing that awkward head-tilt-backward thing to look a man (and often a woman, for that matter) in the eye. But the top of Matthew's head barely came up to my chin, a detail to which he seemed oblivious, yet which immediately made me feel oddly out of place.

How does one look down onto the age-spotted baldness of a giant of faith?

I'm getting ahead of myself. Perhaps it's better to start by telling you I have no explanation for what I'm about to share, other than to say I simply felt compelled to put it down on paper. I realize that doing so will probably land me squarely in the "another California kook" category with some. I also understand that the things that have happened to me are mostly impossible, and that more than a few people are going to assume I've taken a vacation from reality for a while.

Like I said, I have no explanations, any more than I have an explanation for why the sky is blue, or why my ex-fiancé prefers chocolate to vanilla, or why God once glanced out at nothingness and decided that *something* was a good idea. All I've got are my memories, my sketches, my notes. My story. And all I can do is tell you what happened to me. I'll leave it up to you whether or not to believe it. Fair enough?

It all started, coincidentally, on a Tuesday.

CHAPTER ONE

Looking for Moments

I'M A PHOTOGRAPHER, and it's more than what I do. It's who I am. It defines me the way red hair or good looks define other people. And, if you'll pardon my arrogance, I'm one of the best. In fact, sometime in the past week you've probably seen a photo I shot displayed in a magazine, alongside a newspaper story, on the Internet, or maybe even on a billboard or two.

All my photos run under the credit "Todd C. Striker." It's the pseudonym I gave myself when my dad gave me my first camera for Christmas just after I'd turned fourteen. Now I use that name to make a good living for myself—and to keep at least a part of my life private from the outside world. And no, I'm not going to tell *you* my real name either.

In spite of the success I've experienced as a photographer of late, I learned long ago my best images come from hunger. Like the *L.A. Times* award-winning shot of Huntington Beach engulfed in seagulls. I took that one when I was starving—literally. I hadn't eaten since the morning of the day before because I was too broke even to buy a Big Mac at McDonalds. When I got up that day, the gnawing within my gut made me determined to create something I could sell to an editor at the *Times*. A few hours later I found myself at the beach when, out of nowhere, a whirlwind of birds descended onto the sands around me—the right place at the right time. I whipped out my camera and went to work.

That night I didn't go to bed hungry.

Like I said, I'm a photographer. I can't go anywhere without mentally framing the scene in my head. My eyes instinctively act to frame the photo: measuring the light around me, picking apart the colors in the background, and telling my body to move so my shadow doesn't interrupt the scene. And usually, at least once a week—and often more—it all comes together. The world around me slows down, the noises dim, and suddenly the image becomes a split-second freeze that *must* be captured on film.

I've learned to trust that compulsion, to unshutter the 35mm Nikon I always carry with me, and steal the moment for eternity with my lens. At the end of the week, then, I look through all the rolls of film I've shot and find those moments again. They're the ones that typically fetch the highest prices from my clients.

So that's what I was doing that fateful Tuesday seventeen months ago . . . looking for moments.

My journey had taken me to Puente Hills Mall in the City of Industry, where a ridiculous muzak version of the Rolling Stones' "Satisfaction" hummed happily through the walkway speakers.

School was out, but the normal throngs of teen cliques I'd been hoping for had yet to materialize. Instead, there were occasional moms pushing baby strollers, a few elderly people enjoying coffee in the food court, and typical retailers taking breaks and making deals just inside department store display windows.

But the light was perfect. Where I was standing, just above the fountain in the middle of the mall, the light almost glittered with a soft—but demanding—luminescence. I knew it would translate nicely on film.

And I cursed. It seemed almost sinful to watch this light play on the scene without finding a sightline to any object worth featuring in photograph. I was tempted to try to capture just the light, but gave up that idea almost instantly. Light works best when it directs attention to something else, not as the scene-stealer itself.

Then I saw them. They looked young, but not too young. Mid-twenties, maybe. She was a perfect subject—decidedly an attention grabber who'd make just about every man (and many women) do a double take when she walks by. There was an asian beauty about her, with a roundness to her eyes and face that hinted at maybe some kind of Hispanic genes in her bloodline as well.

He was, well, an average white guy. Nothing special about his dirty brown hair, lightly muscled torso, and nondescript T-shirt-and-jeans combination, except that he was standing very close to her. I had to think that anyone who could get that close to her must have some kind of hidden appeal I couldn't see.

It was perfect. They quietly took seats on a bench near the fountain. He opened up a newspaper and started flipping its pages with a calculated disinterest. She simply leaned back and stared carefully into the spraying waters of the fountain. From my perspective on the floor above, the light seemed to intensify around them, and that mental frame I'd been looking for started setting itself up along the edges of my vision. I felt that familiar adrenaline rush and knew it was time to take the picture. The world was slowing . . . I would get their names and contact information afterward, and hope they wouldn't be disagreeable.

I got in position next to a planter and peered through my lens at the couple. But when I focused, I found that her eyes were locked on mine—and she wasn't Asian after all. She was clearly a full-blooded Hispanic woman, with long, charging brown hair and brown-black eyes. She cocked her head a bit and grinned at me through the camera. Average White Guy just turned the page of his paper.

You have to understand, I don't miss these kind of details. A stock of my trade is accurately observing the details. Flustered, I dropped the camera to take another look at the scene. She was still looking at me, still grinning. I felt the freeze frame slipping away.

No, she was clearly Asian, with cropped black hair—but the same brown-black eyes.

She blinked, and then her eyes wandered carelessly back to the fountain. Average White Guy grunted, rolled his eyes, and flipped to the next page of his paper.

I don't handle surreal moments well. I felt my palms start sweating and suddenly heard my own voice muttering to myself.

"Control," I said. "Just let the camera do the seeing." A steely calm settled in, and I aimed the lens again.

Hispanic. Obviously.

I blinked.

Asian. Without question.

My breath started to come in short bursts. I blinked again.

Hispanic.

My finger trembled over the camera's control button.

"She's just playing with you now."

I jumped up in surprise, bumping my knees hard on the planter and letting out a mild profanity before I could think about it. In my concentration on the woman, I'd missed the fact that Average White Guy had moved. He now stood next to me, paper folded up and tucked precisely under one arm.

"Excuse me?" I said.

AWG smiled, friendly, but distant. "Well, at first she was just trying to get your attention. Then she was checking to see which appearance elicited the most receptive response from you. Now she's just enjoying herself." He shrugged. "She's always been a playful sort. No sin, I guess. But it can be confusing sometimes if you don't know her."

I pride myself on taking things in stride, on thinking on my feet. I can even have my eloquent moments. So I stared AWG right in the eyes and spoke.

"Excuse me?"

It was the best I could do. My mind was whirling. Who were these people, and what was going on? I instinctively clutched my Nikon and took a step back.

AWG's smile grew tolerant. "So, do you prefer to be called Todd, or your real name?"

"Excuse me?"

He nodded. "Todd it is then. Todd, do you have a moment for a cup of coffee? We'd love to chat with you, if you've got time."

• • •

"So everybody else died, then?"

I ask the question just to clarify it. In my six-year-old mind, this seems an important point my Sunday school teacher has missed.

"What's that?" Mrs. Fiore frowns in my direction.

"You said the rains came. After Noah had gathered all the animals and his family in the ark. You said the world was flooded, and only Noah had the boat that God told him to build."

"Y-e-s." Mrs. Fiore frowns more, like she's expecting the worst.

"So, everybody else in the world died, then? Drowned? Is that what happened?"

"Well, I suppose so, but that's not what's important. What's important is that God saved Noah and his family, and—"

"Did children die too?"

This is something I need to know. I remember the previous

summer at my Uncle Sawyer's condominium. Our families were spending a day together, and several of us children immediately raced out to the community swimming pool to play. Pretty soon we were happily having splash wars and dunking contests and more. Until my cousin Angela screamed because her older brother, Abel, had tried to "pants" her in the pool.

"You shouldn't do that!" I hollered at Abel. "It's not nice."

"It's not nice," Abel mimicked, laughing. He was 12, and more than twice my size. "Shut up, twerp," he said to me. "She's my sister, and I can do whatever I want."

"But—," I started. Then Abel's big paw was on my head, pushing me down.

"I said shut up!"

I was totally unprepared for the dunking. Water rushed into my throat, up my nose, filling my head. Instinctively I tried to cough, and gulped in more water instead. Panic seized me; I flailed with all my strength.

A second later I felt Abel pull me up by my hair and, through blurred eyes, saw the scared look on his face. I coughed out water all over him, sucking in precious air and spewing chlorine.

Abel got grounded for two weeks. It was two years before I mustered the courage to venture back into a pool again.

And now, with that memory vivid in my mind, I turn back to Mrs. Fiore. "Did God drown all the children too?"

"I suppose so," she says with exasperation. "Now if we can continue—"

"That's a terrible way to die." My voice is louder and more desperate than I want it to be. "What kind of God would murder children like that?"

Rayna Kellogg starts wailing next to me now. "I don' wan' to drown! I hate God! I wan' my mommm!"

Stevie Mitchell's lip starts quivering, and soon he's blubbering too.

"Now see what you've done with your awful questions!"

Mrs. Fiore snaps at me. "You're the pastor's son; you should know better! You, young man, are excused from this class. Now!"

I leave and go sit in my dad's office until church is over, wondering the whole time why God is so afraid of my questions, and if he is, whether or not there is anyone out there who's not afraid of them. It would be nice to talk to that person every once in awhile.

• • •

CHAPTER TWO

The Appointment

"TODD?" AVERAGE WHITE GUY leaned closer. "Do you have a moment for a cup of coffee?

I nodded mutely, afraid to open my mouth and hear another "excuse me" pop out. He signaled the woman—Hispanic now—and soon we were seated in the food court sipping our drinks out of paper cups.

I waited. The woman (thankfully) stayed Hispanic and regarded me through twinkling eyes. Pausing to glance down at herself, she said to AWG, "I think this one will do." He nodded in agreement, and scanned the area around us like a bodyguard searching for snipers.

She suddenly reached out, offering her hand. I shook it, finding her grip firm, yet feminine. "Nice to meet you in person, Todd," she said. "I've admired your work for a long time." She winked conspiratorially. "Particularly that one of Missy in boots and wearing your dad's best hat."

I froze. Missy had been my pet German Shepherd through my teen years. For Halloween one year, I tried dressing her up and took a quick picture of her. It turned out miserably—both for Missy and for me. I'd trashed that silly picture right away. No one knew about it but me.

"Who are you people, and how do you know me?"

The woman chanced a look at her companion. He said simply, "Just tell him the truth. Whether he believes it or not is his problem."

She nodded and turned back to me. "We are servants of the Most High God."

Jesus freaks, I thought. *I'm in trouble.*

AWG stifled a chuckle. "I think 'angels' is a better term than 'Jesus freaks,'" he said. "But you can feel free to call us Jesus freaks if you like." He looked me squarely in the eye. "Either one is better than 'Average White Guy.'"

At that moment I had two choices. I could stand up, walk away as fast as possible and hope these two mind readers wouldn't follow. Or I could employ what the story-makers call "suspension of disbelief" and see where this little encounter would take me.

They waited. I swallowed hard. Finally I leaned back in my chair. "I don't believe this tripe about you being angels," I said calmly. "But, for the sake of discussion, let's suppose it to be true. So what are you doing here, and what do you want from me?"

The Hispanic angel relaxed in her chair as well. "We're here just to set up an appointment. That's all."

"Excuse me?" This was becoming an embarrassing habit.

"Todd," she said quietly. "You've lived practically your whole life with questions—about life, about God, about a lot of things. God has heard your prayers and decided to answer them."

"Huh," I said noncommittally. "You must be mistaken. I haven't prayed in decades."

"Maybe not intentionally," she said. "But your heart prays to God every day, every moment. And for years now it's been pleading with God for someone who isn't afraid of questions. *Your* questions."

My head had that swimming feeling again, but I was determined not to give in to it.

"OK, listen," I said impatiently. "I've had just about enough of this hocus pocus mumbo jumbo where you pretend to know all my deep intimate thoughts. *Nobody* knows Todd Striker but *Todd Striker*, so you can just quit while you're ahead, take your angel butts, and go back to heaven or wherever it is you're really from. Now, if you'll excuse me, I've got a job to do."

They didn't move—didn't seem phased at all by my little outburst. And for some reason, I felt frozen too, waiting to see what would happen next. After a moment, AWG continued as if I'd never said a word.

"Your first appointment is one week from today, next Tuesday," he said. "It'll be just a 'get acquainted' type of affair. We'll pick you up at your house and take you to the meeting place. Dress is casual. Bring samples of your work, if you want. You can discuss how to approach your questions and when subsequent meetings will take place then."

He stood and clapped me on the shoulder. "Meanwhile," he said, "you can go ahead and close your mouth."

She stood too, preparing to leave. I sat dumfounded.

"But who am I going to meet?" I sputtered. "Who, exactly, is this appointment with anyway?"

"The apostle Matthew," she smiled. "See you next Tuesday."

I glanced away for a moment, shaking my head. When I turned back, they were gone, leaving me to wonder what I should do next. Failing to think of anything that didn't begin with a curse word, I followed my instincts.

I took some pictures.

• • •

I can feel the anger ruminating inside me, threatening to bubble over.

It is Sunday school. Again. At nine years old, I've learned—mostly—to recite the right answers and avoid asking too many questions. But this morning is different. Special. Last week my teacher, Mr. Isaacs, brought in a stack of brand new, crisp, bright Bibles. Not just any Bibles, but colorful ones, with pictures on nearly every page and words I actually understood—not those "thou shalt" and "thus saith the Lord" ones.

"So," Mr. Isaacs had said while passing out a sheet of paper with a Bible passage printed on it, "everyone who memorizes The Lord's Prayer from the book of Matthew and recites it perfectly next Sunday will receive a FREE copy of this new Bible just for kids."

I felt excitement at those words. It would almost be like winning a big prize! After class I had sneaked a look at the Bibles, and a hope sprang up within me. Maybe, I thought, maybe I would find answers to some of my questions in this Bible. After all, Mr. Isaacs said it was a Bible just for kids!

Today that excitement has turned sour, replaced by a growing sense of unfairness and anger.

"Well, I have good news and bad news," Mr. Isaacs chuckles nervously to our class. "You all have done wonderfully at memorizing The Lord's Prayer! That's the good news. The bad news is that 11 of you recited it perfectly, but I was only able to find 10 of these kids' Bibles. I had no idea so many of you would want them!"

Slowly, I watch him start passing out the books. "So, since one of our class members is the pastor's son," he says with a nod my direction, "and surely has plenty of Bibles at home, I'm going to go ahead and let the other kids have these Bibles."

I can hold it in no longer. "I want the Bible, Mr. Isaacs," I say quietly. "I EARNED it."

He laughs, nervously. "No, actually, I earned the money to pay for these. They are my gift to the class, and as such, I can choose who receives them and who doesn't."

"But I did what you said, Mr. Isaacs," I say, my voice rising to an embarrassing squeak. "I memorized that passage out of the book of Matthew. I deserve a Bible."

"Now don't be selfish," he says gruffly, giving the last Bible to Ilene Garcia.

"Please, Mr. Isaacs," I say. "How about just the book of Matthew? Can I at least have the book of Matthew from one of the Bibles?"

"That's enough, now," he says. I can tell his patience is wearing thin. "The answer is still no."

And so I break. Leaping on a table I start shouting words I've heard my mother use in private arguments with my father. I demand him to give me that book! I want that Bible! I earned it! My voice has raised to a veritable scream, and my finger thrusts forward at him, aiming right between his eyes. He had promised, I demand, punctuating my fury with more expletives that I didn't even know I had in me. "Give it to me! Give it to me!"

"That's quite enough!" Mr. Isaacs says roughly, yanking me down from the tabletop. "After that foul-mouthed tantrum" he hisses through clenched teeth, "I wouldn't give you the book of Matthew if you were the last child on earth! Wait until your father finds out how you've embarrassed him and his ministry. You ought to be ashamed!"

He surveys me peremptorily. "You are dismissed," he sniffs. "And don't bother coming back next week either."

In my father's office I sit alone once again, waiting for the punishment that's sure to come. I am crying now, but will dry my tears before my father finds me. I will take my penalty like a man. But I vow from this day forward I will never again read a Bible—let alone the book of Matthew.

It's a promise I've kept.

• • •

CHAPTER THREE

Getting Acquainted

I WOKE UP TUESDAY MORNING with bleary eyes and a nauseated stomach. More precisely, I woke up several times on Tuesday morning, dozing off for an hour or two, then waking with a start, certain my so-called angels had come to take me to this mysterious meeting with the apostle Matthew. Finally, around 6:30 A.M., I got so frustrated with not sleeping I decided to get up and try to do something productive like photograph the sunrise or kick a cat. Since I don't have a cat, I opted for the sunrise.

Instead I ended up becoming intimate with the toilet, wondering how I could manage to throw up anything since my stomach had felt empty since about 3:00 in the morning. My body obviously had no such concerns. After a few moments, I made my way back to bed where I lay waiting for the nausea to pass and worrying that those angels were going to knock on my door at any moment.

This is crazy, I thought to myself. *There is no apostle Matthew. That guy's been dead for thousands of years! It's all a hoax, Mr. Striker. Some kind of scam that'll probably lead to a mugging and a lot of embarrassment and hassle. So just roll over, forget all about the psychic-psycho angels, and go back to sleep.*

My eyelids grew heavy, and blissful darkness began to seep in around my consciousness. Just before I dozed off, though, a doubt rang through my mind.

But what if it's real?

That one thought was enough to take the edge off my sleep. My mind began racing with possibilities, and finally my stomach caught up. At 7:25 A.M. I found myself dressed, pressed, pacing my kitchen, and waiting for an adventure.

At 10:45 A.M. I was still waiting, kicking myself for not thinking to ask what time these angel buddies of mine would be showing up.

At 12:30 P.M. I attacked the boredom and frustration of waiting by eating lunch (leftover pizza and a glass of milk).

At 4:10 P.M., feeling like an idiot, I finally gave up, stretched out on the couch, and turned on the TV. I was asleep by 4:15.

At 7:35 P.M. a cool touch to my cheek startled me awake.

"Todd?" she said. "All set to go?"

And there was my Hispanic angel and the Average White Guy, standing as comfortably in my living room as my mother.

"Geez! Don't you guys knock?" I said, wiping a trace amount of drool from my cheek and trying to keep my heart from pounding out of my chest. She just smiled. "And besides, what took you so long? It's after 7:00 at night already!"

AWG shrugged, "We were waiting until you were ready. Why'd *you* take so long?"

"Excuse me?"

"Never mind about him," she said, nodding to AWG. "We've got the car running outside. Shall we go?"

I knew it was crazy to go with these two; possibly even dangerous. And yet something within me knew I could never stay away. If there was a chance that there really was a Matthew, and if he really was waiting to talk to me, I would go. I *had* to go.

I slumped back onto the couch, gathering my energy. "So," I said finally, "do you two at least have names?"

I thought it odd that angels would drive a Toyota, but decided not to say anything. Jackson drove, and Calia sat in the back seat, insisting I take the passenger seat up front. We left my house near Newport Beach and headed north, driving in silence for a while, until I finally asked, "When do you blindfold me?"

"Excuse me?"

I couldn't help but smile when Jackson said it for once.

"When do you blindfold me?" I asked again. "So I don't learn the way to Matthew's secret hideout and stuff?"

Calia's laughter rang like bells. "Oh, Todd," and she sighed sweetly. "You've been watching too many movies. Why on earth would we need to blindfold you?" She reached up and patted me on the cheek, then spoke in a Godfather-style accent, "If we don't want you to find us, you won't. If we do want you to find us, you will." She dropped the accent and shrugged. "That's just kind of the way things work, you know?"

I felt my cheeks get hot with embarrassment, so I nodded and quickly turned my attention to the miles of freeway zipping past my window.

Before long, we were driving down Imperial Highway into Whittier, where we turned down an apartment-lined street and parked at 12222—the Breezewood Arms.

The moon shone like a crescent streetlight in the sky. The night was quiet except for the distant sound of a television set or two somewhere in the packed-in dwellings.

My palms were damp as I checked my pocket and realized I'd forgotten to bring the samples of my work I'd set aside. *Too late,* I thought. *Just have to do without them this time.* Moments later Jackson and Calia had led me up a flight of stairs until we stood before apartment number 23.

We didn't knock; just walked right in. It was a small place, apparently just four rooms: a kitchen, living room, bathroom, and a door to what must've been a bedroom. Jackson poked his head behind that door while Calia stood near me and—as usual—smiled. Then the door opened wide and a man walked out.

He was shorter than I expected. Shorter even than me, and next to Jackson he almost looked silly.

He was healthier than I expected too. I had pictured him as old and weak—after all, he'd been dead for a few millennia. But even though he looked like an older man— sixty maybe—he carried himself with a strength and confidence that surprised me.

And he was wearing sweat pants and a blank-white T-shirt. Not what you'd expect from an ancient disciple of Jesus.

Matthew strode across the room to where I was, raised his hand in greeting and started spouting gibberish in warm, respectful tones. I looked at Calia. She was, of course, smiling.

"He says, 'Welcome, friend. I've heard much about you. Thank you for taking time to meet with me.'" Calia, it appeared, was to be my interpreter for this little rendezvous with history.

My mind raced. "OK, Calia," I said quickly. "Why isn't he speaking English? And why is he wearing sweats and a T-shirt? Shouldn't he be in some kind of robe or tunic or something?"

"Well," she said tolerantly, "He speaks Aramaic—the language of the Hebrews when he lived on earth." She shrugged. "And he was comfortable in sweats, so I told him he could wear them. Hey, the man did die a torturous death simply for believing in Christ. I figure he deserves something comfy. Now, is there anything you'd like to say? Some kind of greeting would be appropriate."

"I need a drink," I muttered to myself. Jackson tapped my shoulder almost immediately while Matthew looked quizzically at Calia.

"Mountain Dew," Jackson whispered as he handed me a glass. "Not what you're used to, I know, but still one of your favorites, right?"

"OK, fine. Thanks," I said, turning back to Matthew and Calia. I didn't hear Jackson leave the room. "All right," I coughed to clear my throat and paused to sip the soft drink. "Please tell 'Matthew' that I said hello. And let him know that while I thank him for meeting with me, I don't really believe that he's some long-dead apostle."

Calia spouted the words back to Matthew, who returned her grin and gave me a long look through twinkling eyes. He spoke, a short, quick utterance that again sounded entirely like someone speaking gibberish with phlegm stuck in the back of his throat.

"He says you want to believe, though."

I frowned. "Yeah, well, tell him I don't believe him anyway."

Calia paused before turning back to Matthew. "Look," she said, "this is going to get awfully cumbersome if you keep saying 'Tell him this; tell him that.' Just talk. And listen. I'll make the interpretation happen; and before you know it, it will be like I'm not even here. OK?"

"Just talk," he said. "And, please, sit down. You look a bit, um, unstable."

"Fine," I said. "I'll sit. And talk. And listen."

He sat in an easy chair and gestured for me to take the sofa. "It's good to meet you, Todd," Matthew said with a contented sigh. "Your father speaks of you often."

"Excuse me?"

He laughed. "Never mind," he said. "So tell me, why am I here?"

"You don't know?"

"Well, I know that I am here, and that the reason I'm here is to meet with you."

I snorted. "I think you're supposed to answer all my lifelong questions, like why the sky is blue and why my ex-fiancé likes chocolate," I said.

The twinkle reappeared in his eyes. "Sorry, Todd. I don't have all the answers. Only God does. But maybe you and I can at least ask some of the right questions."

Something about this guy's voice was getting to me. I could feel my pulse rate slowing. I put down the Mountain Dew and leaned back to finally take a good look at Matthew. He looked back, but didn't speak, comfortable with the silence. I nodded slowly.

"Right," I said. "Well, I suppose we should get to know each other a bit. My name is Todd Striker—but you know that, don't you? Anyway, I'm a photographer, and it's more than what I do. It's who I am . . ."

We spent the next hour or so talking about photography and how I earn my living. Finally he said, "Tell you what, Todd. Let's meet again next week. Same time, same place. And bring some of your work. I'd love to see it." He stood, gave me that same hand gesture he'd used when I first arrived, and quietly excused himself to the bedroom.

Jackson was waiting outside the door when Calia and I walked out. He nodded wordlessly and led us back to the Toyota. I didn't speak on the ride back to Newport Beach. My mind was already busy planning for next Tuesday.

We Talk about Miracles

IDROVE MYSELF TO MATTHEW'S apartment for what we'd deemed was our first "official" Tuesday together. I wanted to make sure it wasn't just some hallucination brought on by those two so-called angels—and I wanted to arrive a little early to check out the neighborhood for anything suspicious.

Matthew and I had planned to meet at 8:00 P.M., so I pulled into a parking spot on the street around 6:55 P.M. I got out, glanced around, and began a little surveillance walk around the tenement. I carried a small folder with a few of my photographs in it. The whole block was a squashed-in community of little apartment buildings that sat inches away from each other: the Scandia Apartments, the Lion's Gate Apartments, Breezewood Arms, and more.

Inside the courtyard of the Breezewood Arms lay a small but clean swimming pool and patio area. The Breezewood apartments ringed the pool in two stories like a rectangular box with the bottom cut out and the sides slapped down to frame the pool. In the back left corner, on the ground level of the rectangle, was a laundry room. In the front right corner closest to the street, on the second floor, was apartment number 23.

I was looking up at apartment 23 when the curtain flew open and Matthew smiled down at me. He waved for me to come up. Moments later Calia opened the door and ushered me in. Matthew greeted me with his usual hand gesture, but this time he held a glass of Mountain Dew in his other hand.

"Peace to you, friend Todd," he said, handing me the drink. "And welcome."

"Sorry, I'm a bit early," I stammered. "Didn't mean to interrupt anything."

Matthew patted me on the shoulder. "I'm just glad to see you," he said. "May I offer you a seat?"

We sat in silence for a few moments. Silence, for me, was always tense. But Matthew seemed to revel in it, waiting, watching, never taking his eyes off mine.

"So, how was your week?" I asked blandly.

He laughed. "Better than yours, I think."

Silence again. Today he was wearing what appeared to be a robe-and-tunic ensemble, with some kind of belt/rope thing around his waist. Definitely a used outfit, but also clean. I glanced up and noticed a pair of sandals carefully placed by the front door.

"Is this more like you were expecting?" he asked, momentarily modeling his clothes. I nodded sheepishly. He shrugged. "The sweats were more comfortable, though. But this is good for today. Next week I think I'll try polyester."

He sat back and waited—again.

As I sat there, waiting with him for who-knows-what, I couldn't help but feel an unusual optimism. Maybe it was seeing him in a tunic, spotting the sandals by the door. Something in me was hoping he was truly an apostle; and if he was, something in me told me I shouldn't waste any time.

"I brought you something," I said, dropping my folder on the coffee table between us.

I laid out four photographs. They had originally run in a

small religious magazine that my father had read . . . well, religiously. It was something of a tribute to him, I suppose, that I even sent the photos to that magazine in the first place. And something of a tribute to him that they agreed to publish them as a photo essay on dying.

"Your father," Matthew said quietly. I nodded again, and turned the first photo toward him.

"Dad, in the early stages of cancer," I said. "The medical treatment left him bald and weak, but at this point he was still confident of a miracle."

My father looked happy in the photo, wearing a loose pullover sweater and jeans, sitting in a recliner with his Bible open in his lap.

I turned the second photo toward Matthew. In this photo my father was thinner but still looking mostly like himself. He was in the chapel of the hospital, kneeling at a prayer bench.

"Dad, when they discovered the cancer had not gone into remission as the doctors had hoped," I said. "He didn't know I was taking the picture until the flash went off. Then he looked up at me and just returned to his business, praying for a miracle."

Matthew nodded, and turned the third picture toward himself. There wasn't much to explain.

"Dad, a week before the end," I said.

He was more a ghost than a man—barely there. The hospital had let him come home then, saying only to make him comfortable for his final days. A home health-care worker had attached monitors and IVs and all those things to my father, transforming his little bedroom into a hospital room. He was sleeping, with his worn-out Bible clutched in his right hand. The brightness of the room was a stark contrast to the dark, wisp of a figure it housed.

"Even then he hoped for a miracle," I said with a weak chuckle.

I glanced up at Matthew and saw moistness at the corners of his eyes. I turned the last photo toward him. It was my father, lying in a casket, Bible spread on his chest. Nothing more to say.

Matthew looked at all four photos. "You're good at this photography thing," he said. "But I don't think that's why you brought me these photos."

"Why do you think I brought them?"

He paused, then said, "You want to know why a loving God would refuse a miracle for your father."

"I know another man," I replied quickly. "Lives in my old neighborhood; attended my father's old church. Eight years before my father got sick, this man also got cancer—lung cancer. He'd been a smoker for years."

"He beat the disease?"

"The doctors said it was a miracle."

Matthew sat back in his chair and put his arms behind his head. Then he spoke, but it was almost as if he were thinking out loud.

"Miracles it is, then. The question is why some experience miracles and some don't?"

I nodded. "They say you've worked a few miracles."

"Yes. Yes I have been the means of some. And seen a few too." His face relaxed into a happy smile. "Tell me, Todd. What are the elements of a miracle? I mean, what makes a miracle a miracle?"

"Well, it supernaturally breaks the laws of natural living."

"Um-hm."

"It accomplishes what previously had been impossible."

"Um-hm."

"And it never happens to me."

"Aah, that's the real question, isn't it? Why don't miracles ever happen to you."

Matthew squinted down at the table between us, then moved with a quickness I found surprising for an older man. Next thing I knew, he had crawled underneath the coffee table and, laying on his back, was squinting up at me through the pane of glass that made the table top.

"Comfy?" I asked, not knowing what else to say.

"Not really," he laughed. "But learning a lot." He inched over to one side. "Come here, Todd."

"Excuse me?"

"Trust me. Be a child again, just for a few moments. Come down here and look up through this table, will you?"

So what do you do when a prophet of God goes eccentric on you? I figured it couldn't hurt, so I joined in. So that's what I did, though I felt much more awkward and clumsy squeezing under the table next to him than he looked when he crawled there in the first place.

"What do you see, Todd?"

"Um, a glass of Mountain Dew. The backs of my photographs. And ... wow. A painting. On the ceiling. In the corner."

In fact, it was an exquisitely detailed painting; a copy of the centerpiece scene from Michelangelo's work on the Sistine Chapel. It was the hand of God reaching out toward the outstretched hand of Adam, the first man. But it was smaller, and tucked away in a corner of the room—on the ceiling.

"Todd, you've been here before. Have you ever noticed that painting?"

"Well, no."

"How about the others?"

"What ... Oh, I see."

In all four corners of the room were small but detailed reproductions of classic art. I'd never even known they were there, and I could only wonder why they might be up on the ceiling of an apartment in Whittier, California.

"Art happens in unexpected places, Todd. The paintings here are in plain view, but it took a change of perspective for you to notice them."

Matthew sighed. "Miracles are like art, Todd. They appear in unexpected places all the time. The better question to ask, then, is why don't we recognize the everyday miracles that happen in life? In your life?"

"What are you talking about?"

"It's all a matter of perspective." Matthew nudged my arm and motioned for me to crawl out from under the table. After we'd returned to our seats, I stole a glance back at the ceiling. Without the magnifying effect of the glass table the paintings were barely noticeable, almost as if the light in the apartment screened out the images to a certain extent.

But Matthew was pointing to something else now. "Look at these pictures of your father," he said. "One moment he was a living, breathing man. Next moment, he was gone, even though his body remained. Death and life, life and death. Don't you see it? The simple act of living is a miracle."

I must have looked skeptical, because Matthew leaned forward a bit. "Think about it, Todd. Have you ever taken a photograph of a newborn child?"

"Yes."

"Close your eyes. Remember one of those pictures. Remember the tiny fingers, the beating heart, the air rushing into the nostrils and animating the body of that child. Why does that heart beat? Why do those lungs breathe? Why does that brain grow active? It's a miracle. The miracle of life. But it's a commonplace miracle, so you take it for granted. You forget it's a miracle of the great Life-Giver himself and cheapen it with your arrogance and ignorance."

Matthew held out his hand toward mine, motioning for me to take it.

"Look at this hand, Todd," he said, pointing to mine. "This hand lives, the same as the child's hand does. Your hand—you—are a miracle."

He leaned back again. I turned my hand over and pointed to a scar that ran down the side of my wrist.

"And yet this seems a pretty shoddy miracle," I said. "This miraculous body has been cut and scarred, sick and broken, weak and useless, and it will eventually die."

"I will tell you of an even greater miracle then, Todd." Matthew spoke closing his eyes. "A miracle I did not see, but which I did experience.

"Once there was a 'shoddy miracle' as you call it that was born into this world. A tiny hand, a tiny heart; cut-able, scar-able; flimsy, weak, and susceptible to illness; destined merely to die. In fact, were it not for the mercy of others it wouldn't have lived past one day. A baby, born through pain and blood and placed, not in a bed, but in an animal's trough."

"Yeah, I get it. The baby Jesus, the Virgin Birth and all. I've heard this story before, you know."

"No, you don't get it," Matthew whispered intently, eyes still closed, as though he were seeing something behind his lids that I could only imagine. "The miracle here is not simply that a baby was born of a virgin."

"No?"

"No. It's that omnipotence would cloak itself in weakness. It's that the miraculous would allow itself to become mundane." He opened his eyes briefly, and gazed deeply into mine.

"The true miracle is that God was *willing* to be born."

Matthew fell silent, and so did I. After a moment he spoke again. "Now I have a question for you, Todd. Why do you suppose God would be willing to do that?"

I had no answer, so I didn't speak, preferring to study the weave on the carpet below my feet. That seemed fine with Matthew, because he didn't speak either. After awhile (I don't know how long) Calia tapped me on the shoulder.

"It's time to go," she said, motioning toward Matthew. He was still sitting in his chair, but now his eyes were closed and relaxed, his breathing shallow and regular. The apostle had fallen asleep on me.

I nodded and stood to leave. "Tell him," I started. "Tell Matthew that I'll see him again next Tuesday."

• • •

It's Christmas Eve, but a far cry from a "silent night." I'm at my father's church preparing for an evening pageant and live nativity scene. As usual, I am dressed in a bathrobe and pretending to be an awestruck shepherd. This year, however, underneath my robe I've hidden the camera my dad gave me for Christmas last year, hoping a photo opportunity will present itself—and that I might be able to sell the picture to our local paper.

Rachel Miller, born only three weeks before, is playing the baby Jesus. Only this baby Jesus has lungs—and judging by the little girl's full-throated screaming and crying, she is feeling quite gassy tonight.

"Elaine," our Joseph says to his Mary, "can't you do something to quiet her down? I mean, we can't have Jesus squalling through the show."

"I've tried everything I know to do, Alan," Mary snaps. "It's going to take a miracle to get this child quiet in time for the show!"

"Then it's a good thing we serve a God of miracles," says a happy voice. It's my father, come in to check on the pre-show arrangements. "It's a full house out there tonight," he says cheerily. "And Rachel will be our star!"

He picks up the baby and swings her around. She promptly spits up on his shoulder, but he just laughs. He hugs her close, ignoring the fact that she's drooling more spit-up on his suit. I see his lips moving close to her ear, but can't hear what he's saying. I know anyway. He's singing "O Holy Night" into the baby's ear, gently patting and rubbing her back. In a moment, little Rachel lets out a belch fit for a Magi.

"What do you know?" laughs my father. "Our first Christmas miracle this year is a burping baby!"

Rachel whimpers a moment or two longer, then droops off into a contented sleep on my dad's shoulder. Mary and Joseph whisper their thanks with relief as Dad gently lays the baby into our makeshift manger.

He seems to forget that he still has a soiled shoulder on his suit coat and wishes us a fantastic show before offering a short prayer of blessing for all us cast members. Then he goes out to greet the audience, and we prepare to go on stage.

The pageant goes without a hitch, but the whole time I am marveling that something as simple as a burp can be a Christmas miracle.

• • •

We Talk about Satan

IFELT LIKE SKIPPING OUT on Matthew when our next Tuesday rolled around. I was cranky, and I knew it. And the thought that he might be dressed in polyester still nagged distastefully at the back of my mind.

I spent the morning at a photo shoot for a print advertising campaign for a line of toys. Some people like "live" assignments with real models better—and of course I've done my share of those too. But I prefer the quiet that comes with photographing action figures or miniature racecars. Nobody blinks at the wrong time; nobody complains about the lights or interrupts the flow of the shoot by proclaiming a need for a potty break; nobody insists I snap only their "good side" or tries to tell me how to do my job. It's just me in a room with blobs of quiet, compliant, colorful plastic.

My ex-fiancé used to tell me I was crazy for craving that kind of solitude in my work. "You'd make double your fee if you'd just do one of those restaurant shoots or even an ad for soft drinks or something!" she'd say. "But you're just too anti-social for that, aren't you?"

She didn't understand. It wasn't the money I wanted when I took a job photographing toys or cars or even chunks of cheese. It was the peace that came with that territory—the precious moments when everything else in the world could be blocked out by the view through the lens of my camera, focused on an object that wouldn't argue or whine or demand anything except my undivided attention. If I could get that same feeling in a live shoot, I'd jump at the chance. But that's not the way this world works, so the morning of our second Tuesday I found myself in the ground floor studio of a toy company in downtown Los Angeles, a boxful of superhero action figures (based on a popular TV cartoon) littered around me on the floor and a table.

I had set the main hero, SuperSol, atop a plastic boulder to show off his sun-inspired powers—a heat ray (OK, orange-colored light) firing out of his glove and a "blinding" sunburst ray streaming from his helmet. His cartoon crime-fighting sidekick, LunaLad, stood next to the rock, one hand on his tidal wave belt and the other readying his "Nightblinder Net" to throw on a few baddies.

The villains were still in the box waiting their turn to pose for the ad when the door opened to the studio and a pale-faced woman stepped partway in.

"Um, Mr. Striker ... ?"

I looked up from the digital camera I was using for this job, a little annoyed at the interruption. She was a middle-aged lady, with a no-nonsense fashion style and (usually) an excessively polite manner typical of receptionists at a front desk. I recognized her as the person who had greeted me when I came in.

"Hello, Diane. What can I do for you?"

"Well ... uhhnf!"

"You can stop talking, for one thing, Mr. Photographer devil!"

That was when I noticed the man pushing his way into the room behind her. He had short brown hair and a wild look in his eyes. He wore khaki pants and a short sleeve dress shirt with a rumpled tie. He shoved the receptionist to one side and quickly slammed the door to the studio shut.

Diane stifled a sob. "Todd," she choked, "he's got a gun."

I froze, and the intruder took a step toward me, flashing the gun into my line of sight with a grin. "Yeah, that's right. Are you scared now? You should be." He took in the scene I'd set with SuperSol and LunaLad and grimaced. "Put the camera down!" he commanded.

"Listen," I said, sounding braver than I felt, "you don't want to do this. I'm just taking pictures of toys here, nothing to—"

He leaned in close, so close I was tempted to try to knock the gun away. But when he cocked the barrel next to my left nostril, I decided against it.

"No, you listen!" he hissed. "I know what you're doing. You and your cohorts here are poisoning the minds of children with this blasphemous cartoon and so-called action figures."

Now I was really confused. "What are you talking a—"

"Quiet! Every thinking person knows that SuperSol and LunaLad are just thinly disguised tools to recruit children into following astrology and eventually into worshiping the sun and moon! But I've got news for you mister: the devil can't have America's kids. Somebody has got to do something to stop you corporate pawns of Satan, and I'm just the guy to do it."

Now it was starting to make sense. The overwhelming popularity of the SuperSol cartoon and affiliated products had touched a nerve among some Christian groups. Several leaders spoke out publicly against the heroes, saying (among other things) that they were a subtle form of sun worship and promoted astrology to unsuspecting children. They also claimed that the two lead characters— SuperSol and LunaLad—represented a homosexual relationship because they shared a hideout and neither had family outside of the other.

The inevitable protests and letters had come, with demands that the show be canceled, that the cards and games and toys and lunchboxes and school folders and such be boycotted out of existence. Some churches, it had been reported, had even held SuperSol burning parties where kids and their parents would turn over their cartoon merchandise to be used for parking lot bonfires. Despite the uproar, the sun-and-moon heroes enjoyed record ratings and generated billions in merchandise accessories. That apparently was what this gunman was unhappy about.

"Put down the camera." He pointed toward the plastic superheros on the table. Over his shoulder, I could see Diane, eyes wide, quietly turning the knob on the door to the studio.

Keep him busy, I thought. *Say something to keep him distracted.*

"Umm, OK," I said. "But is it too much to ask for you to stop picking my nose with that pistol first?"

He snorted a laugh in spite of himself. Then took a step backward to look me over. Behind him, Diane quietly cracked open the door, gave me a meaningful look that seemed to say "I'm going for help!" and slipped through the opening.

The gunman must've read my eyes, because he said, "She sneaked out the door while my back was turned, didn't she?"

I nodded.

"Good," he said, suddenly calm and speaking almost like a rational person instead of a crazed lunatic threatening to insert a bullet in my nasal cavity over a little plastic doll. "What's your name?"

"Uh, Todd. Striker. I'm a photographer."

He snarled a bit then, "I know you're a photographer. I also see you've sold your soul to both the devil and fat wads of cash in exchange for promoting this trash to our unsuspecting children." He cocked his head. "You have kids, Todd?"

I shook my head.

"Figures. You don't have kids of your own, so you don't care if mine go to hell in an astrologer's hand basket, do you?"

He forced a smile. "Well, Todd. I'm a Christian and a reasonable man. I know that pretty soon the police are going to be here, and—hopefully—a few newspaper reporters, all planning to save your sorry life." He paused, and looked at me strangely. "I could do you a favor, you know. I could just end you right now." He waved the gun casually my direction. "But I'm going to give you a chance to repent first. Give you a chance to change sides, to leave your false gods on the table there and come over to God's side."

I swallowed. I'd heard lines like this before, only not accompanied by a gun. "Sir," I said as respectfully as I could, "you are without a doubt an insane man. So could we just get on with this and leave God out of it?"

He grimaced and leveled the gun at my chest. "Put the camera down," he ordered again. After I complied, he grabbed a trash can and thrust it toward me. "Now put that camera and all those evil little idols in here."

Next, he lit a match and flicked it into the shiny plastic garbage.

"That's going to smoke, you know," I said as the flame caught hold. "Might be hard for us to breathe."

A reflection of the firelight flickered in his eyes. "Open a window," he said simply, refusing to take his eyes off the burning toys (and my camera!).

I stepped to the side of the room nearest the street and

cracked open a window, gauging whether or not I had time to jump out before he could shoot me. I pushed the pane up a little higher.

"Todd," a voice said quietly, almost as if it were in my ear. "Duck."

I crouched down, and just then the phone in the studio rang, shattering the isolation of the moment and causing the gunman to break away from the fire in the trash can and look toward the noise. A tranquilizer dart went *ffftt!* through the open window and struck the man right behind the left should blade.

"Aaah!" He jumped in alarm, clawing at his back and inhaling a lung full of smoke from the trash can at the same time. He looked wildly around the room until his eyes settled on me. He raised his pistol and pointed it my direction.

"Todd," the quiet voice whispered again. "Don't say anything. Let the silence speak."

I met the gunman's gaze and waited. He looked hard at me a moment, then dropped the gun to his side with a shrug. "It wuzn' lo'd anyway..." he slurred before dropping to his knees, then to the floor.

"Now!" a voice shouted outside the window, and three armed police officers broke through the door to the studio, weapons trained on the gunman and me. A fourth policeman clambered into the room through the window frame.

"Somebody put that fire out," he ordered. "And cuff that perp before he comes to."

"Jackson?"

The angel/cop looked at me for a second and almost smiled. "Not now. Got work to do. But I'll see you tonight, right?"

More people crowded into the room, and I didn't see what happened to Jackson after that. But somebody did put out the fire, and my next three hours were spent giving reports to the police before I could finally go home. When I got there I found fourteen phone messages—all from various news reporters—asking to interview me about the hostage situation I'd just been through.

Around dinnertime I remembered again that I'd planned to visit Matthew during the evening, but the events of the day had left me tense, cranky, and bit rattled. I decided to skip the meeting this time. Maybe to skip all the rest of them.

My phone rang again and I let the answering machine get it.

"Hey, you've reached Todd Striker. You know what to do. Beep!"

There was a pause on the other end of the line, punctuated by rasping. Then an unfamiliar voice spoke, "He should'a shot you dead, devil worshiper. Repent idolater!" The receiver slammed down to end the call.

I felt the anger begin boiling within me, traveling from my stomach to my fingertips to my temples.

Maybe I would keep that appointment with Matthew after all. And maybe he wouldn't like it. But I was sure going to feel better after I was done telling him exactly where he could put his wacky religion and what he could do with his insane charade about being an age-old disciple of Christ.

I pulled up in front of the Breezewood Arms still angry. I was late for our appointment, but I didn't care. Calia and Jackson were standing outside the door to number 23.

"Exciting day, huh?" Calia greeted. Jackson just nodded.

I stood and stared at them for a moment. Part of me wanted to kick one of them and run away. Instead I changed my mind and turned to leave. Behind me, the door squeaked open and I heard that familiar, guttural language.

"Greetings, friend Todd!" Matthew called out to me. I felt the anger begin to drain from my face. I stopped but didn't turn around. "Wait for me. If you're going to go for a walk, I'd love to join you. We've just enough time before the sun sets."

I chanced a backward glance. As promised, he was wearing polyester—some kind of knit pants and wrinkle-free, patterned dress shirt combination that was either really nerdy or really cool, depending on your perspective. His feet were covered in those same, worn sandals from last week and looked terribly out of place with the rest of the outfit. But he seemed more than comfortable and stepped toward me, inhaling the smoggy air with enthusiasm.

"I wasn't going for a walk," I sighed. "I was leaving."

"Well, wait for me, and I'll leave with you."

Jackson pushed past me and disappeared down the stairs of the apartment building. Calia took Matthew's hand and strolled forward, adding, "Wait for both of us. I'm definitely in the mood for a nice walk."

They both followed Jackson down the steps, and left me standing alone outside the door of the apartment. After a moment, I realized they weren't coming back.

"Hey, wait up!" I shouted, and found myself chasing the people I intended to dump. I caught up with them halfway down the block. Calia had stopped to chat with a few children who were playing ball in the street. When I arrived, she stood up, took Matthew's hand in her left one, and mine in her right, and led the way through a maze of residential streets in the neighborhood.

"So what are we talking about today, Todd?" Matthew asked.

"You don't know?"

He laughed. "Of course not. This is your meeting—your questions, remember? So what's on your mind today?"

I let my mind replay the events of the morning. Then I spoke.

"Satan," I said. "Let's talk about the devil. Beelzebub. Ol' Scratch. Whatever you want to call him."

Matthew nodded thoughtfully. "OK, then. What's the question?"

"Well, today I met a man who saw Satan in a plastic toy, and who threatened to send me to hell because I was photographing the toys for an advertisement. Said he was a Christian and I was an idolater, so I deserved to die."

"Hmm."

"Yeah. You know, Matthew, when I meet a Christian like this guy today, it makes it hard for me to believe in the Christ you talk about. But it makes believing in Satan easier than ever."

Matthew shook his head sadly. "This world hasn't changed much since I was first here."

We found ourselves at a small neighborhood park. Calia led us to a bench and motioned for us to sit down.

"So here's the question, I guess. Why is it so easy to see expressions of the devil in the followers of Christ?"

Matthew nodded thoughtfully, and said nothing—something I found truly irritating. But silence never seemed to bother him, so instead I turned my attention to the orange hues beginning to tint the sky.

"Wish I had my camera," I muttered. "But some Christian burned it in a trash can to save me from hellfire."

I saw Matthew exchange a glance with Calia. After a short nod from her, he held out a hand, palm up, looking into the sky.

"Expecting rain?"

He only smiled and remained focused on ... something.

After a moment, a small spot fluttered into view. As it drew closer I made out the tiny billow of orange and black and watched the butterfly land gently on the outstretched palm of the apostle. It rested there, twitching its polka-dotted wings in slow motion.

"It's beautiful," I said. "Now I really wish I had my camera."

"Take it," Matthew said, holding his hand out toward me. I reached up and he deftly transferred the Monarch to me. "Better cover it up now, or it will fly away."

I clasped my other hand over the top and immediately felt the brush of the insect's wings flapping in the darkness, trying to squeeze out the cracks between my fingers.

Now I realized that Jackson had rejoined us and was, in fact, standing behind me holding a partly singed digital camera. Matthew nodded toward the camera, "I believe that's yours?"

"Yes. Glad to see you saved it, Jackson."

"Great," Matthew continued. "Why not take a picture of that butterfly then?"

"Well, I can't now. If I reach for the camera, the butterfly will wing away."

There was a glint in Matthew's eyes. "Sure you can. Simply crush the butterfly a bit to cripple its wings in your hands. Then you can set it down anywhere and it won't fly away. And you can take the picture."

The thought repulsed me. "Why cripple the beauty of this butterfly just to take its picture?"

"Hmm. I thought you were a photographer."

"I am, but ..."

"If you really are a photographer, then crush the butterfly and take its picture. What are you waiting for?"

"Matthew, I ... are you serious?"

He simply sat back and waited. He was serious ... I think. And we had that dreaded silence he likes so much and I hate so much. So we both waited until finally I shook my head.

"I am a photographer. But I won't damage this butterfly for a picture. Not today."

He nodded, his face giving away nothing of his thoughts. He looked to Calia, and she produced a nature photography handbook and a long stickpin. I realized that the butterfly had stopped flapping inside my hands, and was now walking little steps across my fingers, almost as if it were listening in and trying to get closer to the sound of the conversation.

Matthew flipped open the book, apparently looking for something. He found what he wanted, then read aloud: "Whenever possible, it's best to secure insects to a stationary background for photographing. Of course, this doesn't work for live shots, but is an effective practice when working with insect collections and the sort."

He held up the stickpin. "Here," he said, "I'll pierce the butterfly with this pin. Then you can stick it right to the ground, or on a flower, or tree limb and take the picture."

"No, Matthew."

"But why not? Doesn't the guidebook say to do just that? To secure the insect to a stationary background? It's all right here in the *photographer's* guidebook. Why won't you follow your own rules?"

"It doesn't work like that, Matthew. I don't want to harm this butterfly, can't you see that?"

"Hmm." He nodded to Calia, and I thought he almost smiled. Suddenly we were surrounded by thousands of butterflies, swooping, darting, diving in the air. A dozen or so alighted right in Calia's hair. More landed on my shoulders and in my lap, even atop my hand-prison of their Monarch brother.

"Todd," Matthew leaned in close. "Crush that one insignificant butterfly. Just that one. And I'll give you millions more for your very own. You can photograph any and all of them. Just crush that one."

The beauty of the moment was immeasurable. A sea of orange-and-black patterns, adorned with little white dots. They swept around me in waves, first settling then flurrying across my vision. Every second or so that mental frame would appear and I'd think, what a great photo that would be! Or a quick snap of that scene would earn a pretty penny. Too late I realized the squeezing of my own palms, the sweat that was dripping onto the now-bent wings of my prisoner. The seduction had worked.

I whipped open my palms and saw the butterfly, still alive, but now limping in silent agony, one wing twisted horribly out of shape. I took a look at the waterfall of colors dancing in the sky around me, but they no longer held any beauty or inspiration. They were all mechanical now, tainted by the injury my own hands had caused the delicate creature I held.

Matthew caught my eyes, understanding my remorse. He reached over, scooping the butterfly from my hands and into his. An instant later, his fingers adjusted to reveal the Monarch restored to its original form and glory. It soared from Matthew's palm, joining the carousel of its brothers. A moment after that, the park was empty save for Matthew, Calia, and me. (Jackson always seemed to appear and disappear at will.)

Matthew was wearing a sad smile.

"OK, so what was that all about?"

"You asked why the devil is so often seen in the lives of Christians."

"And that has something to do with butterflies?"

He laughed. "No, Todd. It has something to do with people and the ways that Satan exploits their weaknesses."

Tuesdays with Matthew

"What are you talking about?"

"Three things: pride, religion, and power. Appeals to pride: 'If you are a photographer; If you are really a Christian.' Demands of religion: 'The guidebook says it; The Bible says it.' Power: 'I can give you everything you see.' The devil's tactics involve all these."

"Yeah?"

"Our enemy knows us well."

"You're telling me that's why those who are supposed to be lovers can act hatefully?"

He nodded.

"So that's it then? Ol' horns-and-pitchfork is just too much for Christians?"

"Now for the good news," Matthew said. "There is One who stopped Satan in his tracks. Still does, as a matter of fact. Met him face to face and kicked him in the teeth. The devil appealed to Jesus' pride; he needled him with Scripture that supposedly supported his own demented purposes; even offered Christ all the kingdoms of the earth. But the tempter was no match for the Creator. I wrote all about it in my book. Maybe you remember?"

I shook my head tightly. "Haven't read a Bible in decades," I said, feeling almost embarrassed about it for the first time in years.

Matthew nodded, turning his attention to the spectacular sunset that was now winding down in the western sky. After a moment he stood.

"You know the worst thing about being deceived, Todd?"

I shook my head.

"You don't know you are."

We walked back to the Breezewood apartment arm-in-arm with Calia. Matthew tried to make polite conversation, but I was distracted and, if I am honest, still a bit cranky. I kept feeling butterfly strokes on my fingers, but every time I tried to brush it off there was nothing there.

We stopped at the door to #23. "Next week," Matthew said, "Let's meet earlier."

"Around lunchtime then?"

He nodded, made that now-familiar hand gesture, and disappeared with Calia into the building.

It was midnight before I got home.

• • •

The night is hot. The window in my friend Tony's room is open wide, but the curtains are still. The harsh metal fan blows in the corner, but it seems simply to be swirling hot air currents instead of cool ones.

I am lying on the bottom bunk, sweat sticking to my pajamas, unable to sleep because of the heat. Tony, in his skivvies, is snoring softly through the night.

It is the summer of my eighth year. I had spent the day with Tony and his family at a nearby carnival—riding scary rides, playing arcade games, and generally having fun. Now I am sleeping over at Tony's. Tomorrow my mom will pick me up early, in time to go to church. Tony's family doesn't go to church, and I am envious of that fact.

I am also mad at my friend. Just before we left the carnival, Tony's dad took us to the concession stand and offered us anything we wanted from there. Tony got a large bag of cotton candy. I asked for—and received—the biggest snow cone I've ever seen in my life.

My lips were chapped and dry from the day's heat. My throat scratched, craving the icy sweetness of my new treat. I took one bite, getting colored syrup all over my chin and reveling in the satisfying coolness swimming inside me. Just then, Tony turned without looking and smacked right into my arm.

As if in slow motion, I watched that snow cone fly out of

　　　　　　　　　　　Tuesdays with Matthew

my hand and land in the gritty dirtiness on the pavement.

Tony apologized, but by then the line to the concession stand had doubled, and besides, it was time to leave.

Now, lying in the stifling heat of Tony's room, all I can think about is how my friend cost me the biggest snow cone of my life. And I am getting angrier about it by the minute.

Something flutters on the dresser, caught by an errant breath of the fan. I rise to get a closer look. Tony still snores.

I find that Tony has left a dollar bill and some change sitting unguarded on his dresser.

He coughs, rolls over, and his snore changes to steady, shallow breathing.

He owes me, I think. That was my snow cone. And he ruined it.

Quietly, I liberate the dollar bill from the dresser, leaving the change there.

If he asks about it, I reason, I will tell him the fan must have blown it out the window.

I fold the bill into small crinkles and stuff it into the pocket of my pajamas before returning to bed. The night is still unbearably hot, but at last I drift off to sleep.

And I dream.

In my dream, the sunburned face of a carnival man peers out at me from a concession stand window ... laughing.

• • •

We Talk about Prayer

SUMMER WAS IN FULL FORCE for the day of our next meeting. The stairwell up to Matthew's apartment seemed to capture and magnify the heat of the day, in spite of the shade the overhang provided. I was sweating before I took the first step.

I have to admit I felt a little nervous this time—not because I was meeting with a man who claimed to be a long-dead apostle. I'd gotten past that for the time being. But this day I'd brought Matthew a present.

On Saturday I'd spent the day in Anaheim at Disney's California Adventure theme park. A national magazine was doing a feature article on the park and needed photos of the characters in action, cavorting with tourists and visitors in the park. I was a little surprised they called because I'd never worked for them before. But I was also pleased, because—well, I'd never worked for them before. Anyway, they offered to pay me fifty percent more than what the SuperSol folks did.

Turns out that a key decision-maker in the marketing department for the magazine had read the newspaper story about the SuperSol confrontation the previous Tuesday. "That's the kind of photographer we need," the guy had told his staff. "Somebody who'd stare down the barrel of a gun to get a picture that'd make kids happy ...

And sell a few toys in the process."

They called me on Thursday, then. I didn't have the heart to tell them that it was actually my nostril that had done the staring down the gun barrel, or that my part in the whole episode had been limited mostly to crouching and hoping I wouldn't get shot.

So Saturday morning I found myself walking through guest relations and into Disney's California Adventure, this time with my trusty Nikon for outdoor shots, and also a bulky Kodak with several lenses in a case so I'd be ready if they wanted a studio shot or two in the mix.

It was a great day. The weather was perfect, the crowds were in good spirits, and the characters performed their roles with genuine joy and skill. By 11:30 I had more than enough shots for the magazine folks to choose from. A friendly assistant stuffed a handful of "Disney Dollars" in my camera bag and told me to take the rest of the day off and enjoy the park, on them.

She stayed a moment longer after the others had returned "backstage," chatting lightly, helping me pack up my stuff and secure a locker to hold the camera equipment while I rode the rides. I have to admit I was tempted to invite her to join me for the day. She had a great smile, clear blue eyes, and a trim figure that had turned more than one tourist's head in the few hours of the shoot. But in the end I simply shook her hand, thanked her for the company's hospitality, and walked away. The whole time I talked with her I kept remembering Natalie, even comparing this girl's fingernail polish to the favorites Nat used to wear. It stirred in me feelings I didn't like anymore, and the easiest way to get rid of them was to separate myself from the friendly assistant.

So I did, turning my attention instead to manufactured thrills of the likes of the California Screamin' roller coaster and It's Tough to Be a Bug 3-D movie. Eventually I'd forgotten all about Natalie and the marketing assistant and got lost in the fantasy of a Disney holiday.

After a late dinner, I staked out a spot on the sidewalk to wait for the world-famous Disney's Electrical Parade. I overheard a child nearby jabber excitedly to her parents, "What a great day! I hope heaven is like Disneyland!"

I had to smile at the thought. I hoped so, too. But thinking about heaven also reminded me of my upcoming appointment with one of God's apostles. A few minutes later I strolled past a street vendor selling Disney paraphernalia. On the spur of the moment I peeled off a few Disney Dollars and walked away with a baseball cap featuring Mickey Mouse, Donald Duck, and Goofy smiling at the world.

I'll give it to Matthew, I thought to myself. *After all, he does seem to like contemporary clothes.*

The following Tuesday I stood at the top of the stairs, holding that selfsame cap, and staring at Matthew's apartment door with second thoughts galore.

What if he didn't like caps? What if he took offense at the colorful characters emblazoned on the head? Would he think a Mickey hat akin to idolatry? What if he just thought it was stupid, because—thanks to Calia—he had access to any kind of apparel he wanted?

And why did I care what he thought?

The sound of window air-conditioners whirring in nearby apartments stirred my feet toward Matthew's door. Fumbling a bit with the cap, I rapped loudly next to the number 23. There was no answer. I waited a moment, checked my watch, and knocked again.

Had he forgotten my visit? Did I screw up the time?

"Be right there!"

A woman's voice sang out from the apartment next door. It caught me off guard, and when the door to #24 swung open I was unprepared to respond.

"Hey Jack, you're a couple minutes early, so I ..."

A brunette with ringlets and an oversized purse stopped short in the doorway. She was dressed for work, with a smart-looking skirt and blouse combo that would fit in perfectly behind a jewelry counter at a mall or in the front office of an accounting firm. She was rapidly sliding a pair of heels onto her stockinged feet when she finally looked up and saw me. After a second, the surprise in her face broke into a broad grin.

"Oops! Sorry," she said. "I heard the knock and thought it was my door." She motioned toward #23. "Actually, these walls are so thin that happens a lot. I used to hear the last guy who lived here brushing his teeth every morning. Twenty-two strokes along the top, twenty-four along the bottom."

"Um, sorry for the confusion," I said. "I was just supposed to meet somebody here today. Maybe I'm a bit early too."

She cocked her head and raised an eyebrow. "Here? You must have the wrong place, 'cause that apartment's been empty for over a month now. Maybe you're supposed to be at the Scandia across the street?"

Now it was my turn to be confused. "Empty?"

"Yeah, the last guy moved out, let's see, it was after my niece's birthday so it must have been—"

Suddenly a head popped out from behind the corner of the stairwell. "Hey Miranda! Ready to go yet? I left the car running, and I'm double-parked."

The woman dimpled, "Hey Jack! You bet. I was born ready!" She turned back to me. "You might try the Scandia. I think they have an apartment number 23 too. Cute hat, by the way."

She strode off toward her ride, and I saw Jackson wink at me when she wasn't looking. "Hope you don't mind," he said to her, "but I got a new CD, so we're going to have to sample some jazz fusion on the way."

"Sounds good to me," she said happily. "I just appreciate your willingness to drop me at work on your way to Yorba Linda. My car should be out of the shop tomorrow, so after that you'll be free of me ..." He r voice echoed then faded down the stairwell. A moment later I heard two car doors slam and an engine rev as it drove away.

Empty? How could this apartment be empty if I myself had sat within it several times over the past few weeks?

I turned back to the door, wondering what to do next. Impulsively I reached for the knob and twisted. It turned in my hand, and I felt the latch click from the jamb. Unlocked.

Slowly I opened the door and stepped in, hoping no one would think I was a crook breaking into an empty apartment. It was just as the woman said. Empty. The living room was bare, except for a broom that stood in the corner. The kitchen and dining area was nothing but tile. I checked the ceiling, and even the paintings in the corners had disappeared.

The door to the sole bedroom was closed. I meandered around the living area until I stood in front of it, the whole time trying to decide whether or not it would be appropriate to open it. I finally decided to give up and leave instead. When I turned back, though, I found Calia leaning in the doorway, watching my every move with an amused look on her face.

"He's in there," she said. "He's praying right now, but I'm sure he won't mind if you interrupt. He's grown fond of you, after all."

"What happened here, Calia? Where is everything?"

She glanced around casually. "Oh that. Nothing much, really. I just felt like redecorating in here." She walked over and patted me on the shoulder. "Don't worry, Todd. Jackson'll finish it up for us in no time."

"Greetings, friend Todd!"

I had not heard Matthew come out from the bedroom behind me, but I immediately recognized his familiar, guttural welcome, even without Calia's translation influence. I turned to face him and was surprised when he laid a hand on each of my shoulders and delivered a quick kiss to my right cheek, then my left.

"Where I came from," he said, "that was the way we greeted a personal friend. And I believe we are becoming friends, are we not?"

"Yes, Matthew. I believe we are." I coughed uncomfortably. "But this is how we do it now."

I offered my hand, reached for his, and showed him the typical American handshake.

"Aaah," he said. "I see."

"Men get a little embarrassed about kissing each other nowadays," I said. "Unless they're from San Francisco or something."

"Then handshakes we'll use, friend Todd."

"So, are you hungry?"

His eyes appraised me before he responded. "Not particularly. Are you?"

I felt for a moment that he knew something about me that I didn't want him to know. I changed the subject.

"I brought you something. It's, um, a hat."

"Mickey Mouse, right? Calia told me about him." He quickly donned the cap, slightly crooked and loose, but serviceably nonetheless. Today he was wearing Levis blue jeans and a plain white T-shirt. Same sandals as before.

"How does it look?"

Calia's tinkling-bell laughter filled the room. "At least as good as the polyester, I think," she said.

"Actually," I said while straightening the cap, "better than the polyester."

He patted me on both shoulders. "Thank you, Todd.

I'll wear it proudly."

"You're welcome. Glad you like it."

"So, are you hungry?"

"Well, it is lunchtime, and there is a Del Taco not far from here. I thought, if you wanted, maybe we could hit that place for a quick bite."

He got a puzzled expression. "I'm not sure I know what a *delitokko* is, but if you recommend it then I'd be happy to join you."

"Not *delitokko*. Del Taco. It's a fast-food Mexican place."

"Mexican?"

"Never mind. It's just a place that serves good food."

"Then let's go."

The restaurant was crowded when we got there, so Calia and Matthew scouted a table while I stood in line to order. Since they weren't there to instruct me as to their preferences, I bought three of everything I liked: chicken burrito, basic taco, and Mountain Dew to drink. We divvied up the food at the table. Calia and I started unwrapping the food, but Matthew just pushed his to the side a bit and leaned forward on the table. I took my first bite, then a second before I noticed that Calia hadn't started eating hers yet either. Both of them sat, looking at me with question marks in their eyes.

"Everything OK?" I said.

"Yes," the Apostle responded. "Smells delicious."

Great.

I took another bite and noticed that neither of them had followed suit. Finally it dawned on me.

"Oh. You know, I don't do that. So, I mean, you can feel free to do it for yourselves, but ..." I shrugged.

"Do what?" Matthew asked.

"Well, pray. Before meals. Or anytime really."

Calia looked at me tolerantly for a moment, then began eating her burrito. Matthew nodded.

"Don't think I even know what words to pray anymore." I shrugged again, and tried an unconvincing grin.

Matthew leaned back. "Sometimes the best prayers are the ones without words anyway. But I can give you some words to pray, if you want."

"Knock yourself out. But, really, I don't—"

Calia's hand stopped me mid-sentence. She jabbered a bit in Matthew's language, until he nodded, then turned back to me. "Sorry," she said. "Had to explain what 'knock yourself out' means. Now, let me get out of your way ..."

"He taught it to me himself, you know. But it's more than just words. It is the heart of a prayer, expressed in phrases."

"Like I said, knock yourself out."

He rambled the words comfortably, not with the same grandeur or posturing I'd heard others recite the prayer before. For Matthew, it was if he was speaking to a close friend, not quoting an age-old, world-famous prayer.

"Our Father in heaven, hallowed be your name. Your kingdom come, your will be done on earth as it is in heaven. Give us today our daily bread. Forgive us our debts, as we also have forgiven our debtors. And lead us not into temptation, but deliver us from the evil one."

"I remember that prayer."

"And ...?"

"It's been a long time."

"And ...?"

"Well, to be honest, it seems to me like prayer just doesn't work."

"So that's today's question, then?"

"Well, OK. Yes. Let's talk about prayer. Why is it so important? What good does it really do? I mean, Christians have been praying your prayer for thousands of years, but is God's will really being done 'on earth as it is in heaven?' I don't see it, at least not in Los Angeles. Will there be no Christians who go to bed hungry tonight—even after praying for God to provide their 'daily bread'? And, after last week, you and I both know that temptation still floods the lives of Christians and non-Christians alike. Besides—God's going to do what God's going to do. So what's the point? Why pray? Why does God even want us to pray?"

Matthew nodded and pushed his food away once and for all. "Let's find out."

He stood up, taking my arm and dragging me out of my chair at the same time.

"Pretty good grip for an older guy," I teased. "Where are we going?"

The Apostle didn't respond. Instead he walked me over to a table where three college-aged kids—one guy and two girls—were chowing down on burritos and tostadas. They looked up at us.

"Hey, can I help you?" one of them said—the guy with sunglasses and dark, bushy hair. "Need some extra taco sauce or something?"

"Ask them," Matthew said.

"What?"

"They can't understand me. And Calia's still back at our table, so she can't interpret."

"Then how can I understand you?" I said, glancing back to see Calia take a thoughtful sip of her drink.

"Oh, herald angels tend to be very good at their jobs. She has ways of communicating that you'd never believe."

"Dude, is there a problem or something?" The young man flipped his sunglasses up on his forehead while the two ladies exchanged raised eyebrows.

"Are you foreigners? From another country?" asked the blonde girl. "Maybe they need help ordering or something."

"No, um, sorry." I said. "Well, he's from, uh, someplace else, but ..."

Matthew nudged my shoulder. I sighed.

"Actually, my friend here—his name is, uh, Matt—he wanted me to ask you a question."

The three students shuffled in their seats, waiting. Matthew poked me in the shoulder again.

Finally I just blurted it out. "Why do you pray?"

"You mean, why did we pray over our food before we ate?" The redheaded girl had joined the conversation now.

"Yeah. Well, no. I mean, why do you pray, ever?"

The redhead elbowed the one with sunglasses and moved over on her bench. "Why don't you guys sit down."

Matthew started to park himself on the bench, but I stopped him. "Uh, no. We don't want to interrupt whatever you all are doing. Just wanted to ask the question is all. We'll be going now." I started to pull the Apostle away.

"Dude, you asked the question. At least give us a minute to think about an answer."

The blonde spoke up again. "Well, I don't know about you two," she said, motioning to her friends, "but I guess I pray because I need to. Something within me needs to cry out to God. So I do it, and I feel better, regardless of the answer."

The redhead added, "Yeah, I guess that's true. And I need to know that Someone bigger than myself is listening. Someone who actually cares, and can do something about whatever I'm going through."

Sunglasses looked at me with a twinkle in his eyes. "Actually, I just pray because it's free, and on my budget anything free is a good thing!"

The girls laughed, and even Matthew seemed to get the joke. "Thank you. That's great. Thanks. We'll just go back to our table now."

"Dude," Sunglasses grabbed my wrist. "All kidding aside. Would you like us to pray for you?"

I felt redness flushing up my neck and into my face. "No. No thanks. Really. Thoughtful of you though, but, no. Thanks."

Back at our own table, Matthew gave me that appraising look of his. "You should have let them pray for you."

"Why? So I could be embarrassed further, right in the middle of Del Taco?"

He laughed. "No. Because they're praying for you anyway." I stole a look back at the college kids' table. They were indeed praying. Holding hands, with heads bowed and eyes closed.

"Whatever."

There was silence for a moment. Then Matthew spoke. "Tell me more about your dad, Todd."

"What's that got to do with our topic for today?"

"Just tell me about him. Anything. Any memory that brings him to mind."

An old, but clean, station wagon with wood paneling leapt into my mind.

"OK," I said. "I remember his car. It was brown, and big, and squeaked every time he took a sharp turn."

"What else?"

"I remember … I remember waiting for that squeak to come every Friday after school in sixth grade. My mom had a women's group meeting on Fridays, so Dad would leave the church and come get me."

"Don't stop."

"What's this got to do with ..."

"Don't stop."

"Well, Fridays were my favorite afternoons. I'd sit on the curb outside the school and wait, loaded down with books or whatever—ready for the weekend. And every Friday, without fail, Dad would squeak his car into a parking place and motion for me to jump in."

"Then what?"

"We'd drive home. No, that's not totally true. We'd drive around until mom's meeting was over. Sometimes we'd get ice cream. Sometimes we'd go to a park, or run a few errands. He'd ask me about school and homework and sports, or what was going on with my friends or about the clubs I was in at the time. He'd check to see if I needed his help with any homework for the weekend, or if I needed school supplies or sports equipment and stuff. Sometimes he'd take me back to the church to help him out with some project. Mostly we'd just hang out together, I guess, talking and doing whatever the day required."

"Did your mother's Friday meetings last all that school year?"

"You know, now that you mention it, I don't think they did. In fact, I think they only ran for about six weeks, right at the beginning of the school year."

"Did your dad stop picking you up, then?"

"No. I never really thought about it, but he picked me up every Friday that whole school year—rain, sleet, wind, or snow."

"Why?"

"I guess he wanted to spend time with me."

"Even when you were in a bad mood? Or when all you did was wheedle him for some new toy, or dump your day's problems on his shoulders?"

"Yeah. I guess so."

"Did he always give you everything you asked for?"

"Huh! No. Not even close."

"Yet he always showed up when you asked him to, right?"

"Ye-es. I think I see where you're going with this."

"Then why don't you tell me?"

"My Fridays with Dad weren't about what we said, or even what we did. They were about us. About making time for each other. About being involved in each other's lives. About helping each other to go through another day. About growing closer to each other, in rain, sleet, wind, or snow."

"Todd? When was the last time you spent a 'Friday' in prayer with your heavenly Father?"

I didn't answer. I couldn't remember the last time.

"Seems to me that prayer is more than just words, or a checklist of things you want God to do for you. Seems to me that prayer is a Friday afternoon, riding around with your Father, talking about the things that are important to you—that each moment in prayer is a chance for you spend time together, to get to know each other better. And that's the real answer to prayer—intimacy with God, regardless of how your circumstances change as a result of praying."

"I miss my Dad, Matthew."

He reached across the table and patted my hand. "And your Father misses you, Todd. And he hears the prayers your heart speaks even when you don't intend to pray. Why else would he send me to reintroduce you to him?"

We sat among the stained burrito wrappers for a few moments more, each lost in our own thoughts. I didn't see my college buddies leave, and barely noticed as the lunch crowd thinned out. Finally I spoke.

"I'll think about it, Matthew. I'll definitely think about it."

I dropped Calia and the Apostle at the curb outside the Breezewood Arms. "How about breakfast next Tuesday," I suggested. "Around eight o'clock or so?"

"It'd be a pleasure, friend Todd. Peace be to you until then!"

I drove toward home, already looking forward to next week. And also wondering why Matthew hadn't touched any of his food or drink during our time together. Those thoughts kept me up until late into the night.

• • •

"Oh God, oh God, oh God!"

"What are you doing?"

"What does it sound like I'm doing? I'm praying—and you should be praying too! Oh God, oh God, oh God!"

I hear the gravel crunch under my feet and sneak a sideways peek at my date.

"It sounds more like you're hyperventilating."

"Very smooth. Bet you say that to all your girlfriends just after you wreck their cars and leave them stranded in the night, miles away from any phone. Oh God, oh God, oh God!"

I grin in the darkness. "Well, I figured that fender bender already cost me a goodnight kiss, so I wasn't going to lose too much saying it."

"Todd, this is serious. My dad's going to kill me for letting you drive my car. And look at the road—we're in the middle of nowhere!"

I want to say something smart then. Funny, yet sensitive. Reassuring. To be honest, I am still hoping for just a little smooch on the porch when this is all over.

Instead I feel my feet go numb, and could swear someone is pumping helium into my brain. When I open my eyes, my first thought is that the stars are beautiful—and that there are millions of them. My second thought is a curious query to myself:

How did I end up on the ground?

"Oh thank God, thank God thank God!"

"Sonya?"

She is crying now. "Oh Todd, you passed out. I didn't know what to do. Can you hear me? Can you understand what I'm saying?"

I want to nod, but suddenly I have a very bad headache. It hurts to blink, so I just shut my eyes and mutter, "Not so loud, Sonya."

"Todd, we've got to get you to a hospital. I think your head is bleeding—I-I can't tell for sure in the dark. Todd, you've got to stay awake. Oh God, what are we going to do?"

"God? Ouch!"

I feel Sonya's hands pressing something soft on the side of my head—and it sends a sharp pain throughout my nervous system.

"Oh Jesus, please help us. Todd, I know this hurts, but I've got to stop the bleeding. I'm pressing my sweater on the cut."

"Gon' ruin your sweater."

"Todd, just shut up a minute. But stay awake!"

We are both silent. I feel the minutes slip by. In the silence I hear Sonya, whispering now. "Oh God, sweet Jesus, we need you. Please, please, Jesus, please help us. Please send help. Please ..."

I think I pass out again, but can't tell for sure. But now there is a light on the road and Sonya is screaming. The light grows brighter, then stops close by. The pain in my head throbs. Why doesn't somebody turn out that blinding light?

I hear a roaring in my ears. Or is it a siren?

Strong hands grab me, roll me onto something flat and hard. The light finally goes out and I can see millions of stars once again. When I next try to open my eyes, I can't because some sort of bandage covers them.

I hear Sonya sobbing.

"Don't worry, miss," a kindly voice says. "He's going to be

just fine. Lucky someone saw you two wrap that car around that tree, and then called us right away. And lucky our ambulance was already nearby to boot. Somebody up there must be looking out for you two."

I hear Sonya softly praying again. "Oh God, oh thank you God, oh thank you God ..."

Maybe I'll get that kiss after all. Thank God!

• • •

We Talk about Purpose

THE SMELL OF HASH BROWNS smothered with onions and pepper sneaked through the cracks in front of apartment 23 the next Tuesday I was there. I stood at the door and breathed deeply. It was a nice smell—one that reminded me of home. I was glad I'd thought to bring along a jug of orange juice (with pulp). It was just too early in the morning for Mountain Dew.

The smell of food also made my heart speed up just a tick or two. So far, I'd met with Matthew each week for a month, and in none of those meeting had he ever so much as nibbled on a cracker or sipped at a cup of coffee. I didn't even notice it at first, but when he'd left all his food untouched the last week at Del Taco, a nagging suspicion began to ruminate in the back of my mind. I spent a few hours Saturday at the library doing a little research, then, and based on a quick overview of the subject, my suspicions seemed valid ... and idiotic at the same time.

Still, so far this had been an experience that was inexplicable, and this idiotic notion at least offered some kind of rationalization. And that was another reason why I'd stopped off to pick up the OJ on my way over to see Matthew this morning. It was silly, but it was one small test that I could run to ease the confusion in my mind. So I prepared to do it.

The surface of the door to Matthew's apartment felt cool to my knuckles, even though the morning sun was already beginning to make its presence known among the cramped-in dwelling. I tried to knock a bit more softly this day. No need to wake up Miranda unnecessarily.

Jackson swung open the door, gave me a half smile and nodded for me to come in. Matthew was standing on the edge of the dining area, holding a few plates in his hands and looking back into the kitchen where the delicious smell was wafting generously into the air. Today he wore what I can best describe as long pajamas, or maybe an adaptation of a Japanese kimono, I'm not sure. The shirt was long—almost knee-length—straight and silken, with splashes of color over a pale red background. The matching pants hung loosely down his legs, allowing padded slippers to peek out from under the cuffs each time he moved. I have to admit he looked both stylish and comfortable, and I was tempted to ask where I could pick up something like that for myself.

Calia was saying something from in the kitchen, but it was in that unintelligible language of Matthew's, and I couldn't make it out. The Apostle responded promptly, though, nodding and turning to arrange the plates on a brand new table in the tiny little dining area. He paused to grin and nod respectfully in my direction.

"Like the new look in here?" Jackson asked. "Took me a while to find just the right color of paint for the walls; but once I did that, everything seemed to fall into place."

I must confess that for an interior decorator, the angel had a ... *unique* style. The living area seemed a swirl of colors and civilizations. A Japanese futon rested carelessly next to a Victorian era wingback chair and a pillow-topped, plush wooden bench. A director's chair sat folded up in the corner, and the glass coffee table had been replaced by a chrome-and-metal piece that looked more modern art than a piece of furniture. The central feature of the dining area was what appeared to be a finely hand-crafted table made of a rich mahogany wood. Its surface was smooth and silky to the touch, but the table legs sported intricate carvings that apparently depicted scenes from biblical history. Surrounding the table were four matching mahogany stools, each with a smooth top sur-face and spinning designs down the legs. A peek into the kitchen revealed a thoroughly modern, American place, complete with microwave, stove, refrigerator, and even an electric can-opener bolted to a counter.

But it was the walls that really caught my attention. The paint Jackson had used was like nothing I'd ever seen before—a milky bluish color with a shadowy tint that looked almost like someone had taken the sky, several clouds, and a bit of a star and mixed it all together in a blender. It had an eggshell finish that gave it a rough tex-ture, but when I reached out to touch it, it felt more like silk than paint on a wall. There was a luminescence behind the paint as well, almost as if the sun had risen behind the walls and was now lighting them from within. Involuntarily, I checked the corners of the ceiling in the living room, and Jackson laughed.

"Painted over them," he said. "But keep checking. You never know when the impulse to imitate the art of the Creator may overtake me."

Calia stepped out from the kitchen with Matthew at her side, both laden with foodstuffs of a morning. The Apostle carried a large pan of scrambled eggs and a spatula. Calia delivered a skillet of hash browns and breakfast rolls to the center of the table, now set with all modern flatware.

"I see you brought juice, Todd," she said in greeting. "Good. Then let's eat!"

We sat at the table and the rush of savory smells reminded me that I'd skipped breakfast that morning—

and that I was now very, very hungry.

"Wow," I said. "Who knew angels could cook?" I motioned to the apartment walls. "Or decorate apartments, for that matter?"

Calia's tinkling laugh filled the room. "Oh, we're versatile." She looked at Matthew, and he nodded in response. Raising his eyes toward the ceiling, he began speaking in Aramaic, apparently saying a prayer before breakfast. For some reason, Calia didn't interpret this time, and when he looked down again all eyes fell to me.

"What?" I said. "Did I forget something?"

Calia nodded toward Matthew. Deliberately, he reached for a utensil and plunged it into the pan of hash browns, pulling out a healthy forkful of fixings. Never loosening his gaze from mine, he stuffed the helping right into his mouth, chewed carefully, and swallowed.

I felt my face flush a little red.

Matthew just grinned, reached over, and took a sip of juice from his glass. Afterward, he opened his now-empty mouth wide and leaned over so I could get a closer look inside. (Not an entirely pleasant sight to stare down the throat of anyone, particularly an older gentlemen who was once a great prophet of God.)

Calia and Jackson both let out stifled chuckles, stared at me, and waited.

"Calia told you, didn't she?"

He regarded me with a fatherly expression and nodded. "Yes, she did, friend Todd. I thought it was funny at first, but Calia indicated it was a serious concern for you, and Jackson suggested this would be the best way to reassure you and thus remove that distraction from our time together."

"I'm sorry. It's just that I've never met a dead man before. And you never ate anything, something the books say is the sign of an immaterial spirit being. And ..."

He reached across the table and clapped me on the shoulder. "It's understood. But so we are clear on this matter: I am certainly not now, nor have I ever been a ghost. There is so much delusion in your society regarding the spirit world, and so many ways the enemy has twisted the truth to fit his lies, that it's no surprise you might be swayed by that thought. But it's just not true. I am exactly who you see here, in the flesh just as you are now and just as I once was many, many years ago."

I stood up, forgetting the hunger roiling in my stomach.

"But ... *how?* How can that be? It's crazy. Does that mean I'm crazy?"

"No, Todd. Sit down. You're not crazy, and the fact that I'm here isn't crazy either. Unusual, yes. But not crazy."

"Then what is it?"

"A miracle," he said simply. "They happen more than you admit. God has moved heaven and earth—literally— to work this miracle for you. You don't need to explain it. Just take advantage of it. While we have the time."

"How much time do we have?"

Matthew shrugged. "That's not my decision to make. But I am here today, so let's take advantage of that, shall we?"

I nodded, thoughtful. Jackson and Calia started eating their own breakfasts then, so I joined in.

"Well, what are we going to discuss today?"

"I think that's up to you, isn't it?"

"OK, let me think about it while we eat."

After breakfast, Jackson excused himself and stepped outside, scanning the complex on his way out. Calia, Matthew, and I retired to the living room where the Apostle flopped comfortably on the futon while Calia and

I took seats on the bench.

"Matthew," I said, "here's my question today: Why are you here, really?"

"Because of you."

"No, I mean, what's your purpose for being here?"

"I think what you really mean is what's *your* purpose for being here. What is it that God has planned for you that makes it so important he would send me to be here with you? Isn't that right?"

"I didn't ask that."

"Yes, you did. You just didn't say it out loud."

I looked disapprovingly at Calia. Matthew laughed. "It doesn't take an angel to read that in your face, Todd."

"Well, Matthew, the question I'm asking you out loud today is about you. What's your story? How did you get from where you started to this place today? And, OK, I'll admit that maybe I'm hoping to learn something about my own purpose by hearing about yours. But I also just want to know more about you, about your past, about who you are. Will you tell me?"

He sighed. "My story isn't what matters, Todd. It's the story of Jesus Christ that—"

"Matthew. Right now it's your story that I want to hear. Will you tell me? Friend?"

From somewhere I couldn't see, Calia produced a sketchpad and a few pencils. "Here, Todd," she said.

"What's this for?"

"Your best camera is in your eyes. I thought you might want to have sketches of this time. Later."

"I haven't done much drawing since college."

She shrugged. "You don't have to sketch now, Todd. I just thought you might want to. If you don't, then don't."

Matthew, waited patiently through my exchange with Calia. Then he spoke. "OK, Todd. This is your time. You asked a legitimate question, and you deserve an answer.

I can't tell you my entire story, but I can tell you some."

He leaned forward in his seat, assuming the role of a griot, as if he were an old teller of tales rehearsing a history that would be lost if it were not passed on verbally to younger generations. He began speaking in third person, relating his story as though it were someone else's.

"I will start at the place where Matthew's day drained away for too many years. At a tax collector's booth now lost in history ..."

Matthew wiped the sweat forming on his forehead, never noticing the dust and dirt that had accumulated on his hand, and which now left a dark smear across the line of his right eyebrow.

"More," he said firmly, never taking his eyes off the stack of coins that teetered tantalizingly on the table in front of him.

"Please," the merchant said piteously, "I have five children and a sick wife. We truly can spare no more!"

The smudge above Matthew's eyebrow arched in appraisal. He quickly calculated the value of the silver coins in front of him. There was enough to pay the Romans, all right. But barely any left over to line Matthew's silken pockets. After all, a man of his position had expenses. And this merchant had to pay his part. Besides, hadn't the merchant packed his carts with spices and salt to sell in Matthew's precious Capernaum? He stood to profit from entry in this city. It was only fair that Matthew also share in that profit.

He licked his lips, feeling the dryness and tasting the familiar grime of the day. Anyway, he didn't like this prattling merchant. Didn't like anyone, really. That was one drawback of collecting taxes for King Herod and the Roman oppressors. It inevitably made you an enemy of those who put patriotism above a wealthy lifestyle. And it seemed like there was an endless supply of those distasteful people. Well, they didn't like him, so he returned the favor.

"More."

The merchant laid four more coins on the table, wailing all the time that Matthew would make him bankrupt—or worse. It was enough, all that Matthew had asked for in fact. But now the glint of silver and the irritation of enduring this man's ceaseless whining took control.

"And a tenth of the cinnamon on your cart."

"What? You wretched little thief! You've taken my money and now you wish to take my livelihood as well? Never! Pigs don't deserve cinnamon. Let them wallow in the dirt where they can eat their fill of refuse. You may hang me from the highest branch or crucify my children, but I'll never pay you more than what I already have!"

Matthew stood. "Hanging and crucifixion can be arranged," he said. He made a motion toward two Roman soldiers guarding the entryway to the city gate. They strode to the merchant, who now cowered in fear. One soldier drew his sword and swung the flat part of the blade against the merchant's right temple. He crumpled to the ground, whimpering.

Matthew walked around the table and knelt close to the merchant's ear. "Now, dog, I will take 15 percent of your cinnamon. And two more silver coins. Unless you object?"

"N-no. I will pay. I will pay."

The soldiers laughed and returned to their post. As they passed, Matthew pressed a silver coin into the palm of the leader, and then waited patiently while the merchant unloaded the cinnamon into a storage area behind Matthew's table. "Next!"

Matthew had no problem collecting taxes for the rest of that day.

It was at nighttime the problems came. When his eyes were open, Matthew could endure the hateful stares and whispered curses people shot his way. When his eyes were open he could spit on the insults and sneers his fellow countrymen heaped on him, ignore the way people called him a traitor, lumping those of his profession with that of murderers and thieves. Even a prostitute had a better reputation than a tax collector. But Matthew had soon discovered that a man with money doesn't need friends, or praise from the masses, or even a country to call his own. All he needed—all he wanted—was enough wealth to live comfortably and to punish his enemies.

Still, it was at night when the sickly sweet smell of burning incense mingled with the memories of the day, when Matthew would lie down in his comfortable bed and allow his eyelids to close—the night was what made life difficult. That was when the voices calling him traitor changed to something more familiar, when the derisive faces and glaring hatred that oppressed his life reflected the feelings of Matthew's own heart. And in his nightmares, no matter how much money he tried to pay, the hardened face of his accuser would never relent ... for it was his own face.

More than once his groans pierced the night. *Oh God ... who will save me from myself ...*

Yet every morning, the richness of his wine and the sumptuousness of his breakfast table made the agony of the night before fade. And so each day he took his position at the tax booth by the city's entrance, licking his lips, sweating in the grime, growing richer with every new "customer" who passed through.

It was on a day such as this that Matthew discovered his true purpose in life. Already he'd collected a nice bounty of silver coins, flour, wheat, and even a smooth piece of ivory he couldn't resist. In his mind he was preparing for a party, a gathering of other tax collectors and "sinners" at his house to celebrate the wealth of his position. They were not friends, of course. But they shared his fate and thus were more than happy to share his food when it was offered.

There was something of a commotion that distracted Matthew from exacting his tax.

"It's the Rabbi! He has come to Capernaum!"

Matthew watched as onlookers in the marketplace rushed to get a glimpse of this rabbi. Certainly he wasn't worth losing out on silver and spices! He turned his attention back to the table and demanded two more coins. The merchant pleaded for mercy (they always did, it seemed), and Matthew sighed.

Out of the corner of his eye he caught sight of a peculiar movement. Was the rabbi's procession going to pass right in front of this booth? Absurd! Matthew had work to do, and while he respected many religious leaders, he would not allow any interruption in his accumulation of wealth.

Suddenly the air stilled around him. Silence fell over the marketplace, and he felt as though all eyes had suddenly turned to him.

Matthew looked up from the sparkling coins on his table and caught his breath.

A man—the Rabbi—stood before him. It was not all eyes gazing on Matthew; it was the Rabbi's eyes, and in them the tax collector could see the eyes of heaven staring into his soul.

It was almost like nighttime again, there in the middle of the day. The accusing voices inside him breached their defenses and shouted "Guilty! Guilty!" into his ears. Memories of greedy theft and abuses of power flashed through his mind. The pain was nearly unbearable, and Matthew wanted to cry out, to run from those eyes that pierced and convicted and shoved the unblinding truth out into the open.

"Who are you?" the tax criminal whispered, trembling in spite of himself.

The Rabbi said nothing at first, only took a moment longer to gaze into his quarry's eyes. Then he smiled, and in the shadow of that smile Matthew found erasure, heard the guilty voices being choked into silence and a new voice murmuring "Forgiven ... forgiven ... forgiven ..." into his ear.

The Rabbi finally spoke. "Follow me."

Two words that changed the destiny of a criminal, a traitor, a thief, a liar. Two words were all it took. Matthew felt hope swelling inside him. Anything. Everything. All of him. That was his purpose. To take every iota of his being and place it in this Master's care. To follow him, no matter where, no matter when.

Silver, spices, even ivory was forgotten. Matthew had no second thoughts. He left it all behind, got up, and followed him.

"And that, friend Todd, is my story. That's is when I met Jesus Christ, when he invited me to follow him. And when I finally found purpose in my life that carried me through to the end of my days."

"I never knew," I replied. "I mean, I knew you had been a tax collector. But I never knew ... well, you know what I mean."

"Todd, you told me once that you are a photographer, and that it was more than what you do, it's who you are."

"Yes?"

"I am a disciple. That is who I am. That's the only place I've found to have true meaning in this life, as Christ's disciple."

"I see."

"I hope you do see, one day, Todd. I truly hope you do."

We sat in silence for a moment—something I was learning to appreciate more and more, thanks to Matthew. In my hands I rediscovered the pencils and the sketchpad.

He'd been easy to draw, really. I almost hadn't even had to look at him. His voice had seemed to guide the picture in my mind, and all it took was for me to copy what my mind's eye was seeing. Now I realized there were two faces on my page. One of Matthew as a young man, hardened, with the prize of silver glinting in his eyes. The other of Matthew as he was now, strong yet gentle, with a wisdom I so longed for but that seemed never to be within my reach.

"Very nice, Todd." Calia admired the sketches over my shoulder. "Better than I expected, to be honest. Can't wait to see what else you might draw."

I felt embarrassed to have an angel checking out my drawings, so I slapped the sketchpad closed and changed the subject. "Well," I said, "somebody's gotta' do those dishes, and it might as well be me."

Calia jumped up from the bench. "I'll help you." She patted Matthew on the shoulder. "Why don't you go rest in the bedroom for a bit?"

He stood and nodded, offered me his hand for a handshake and spoke that same Aramaic greeting I'd come to recognize.

"Yeah, Matthew. I'll see you next week."

• • •

"What is the purpose of the clay?"

Mr. Houlihan's booming voice rings out across the classroom. It is a friendly voice, but one not suited to the confines of a seventh grade art class. There is no way to lower the volume, making Mr. H one of our favorite teachers to imitate (behind his back of course).

He slaps a block down in front of Kerry Washington. "Is it to be a beautiful piece of pottery sold for riches and admired by many?" He grins and lobs a glob toward Isaac Jones. "Or is it destined to be a brick hidden away in the deep recesses of a forgotten building?"

He continues passing out the apportioned amount of clay to each. When he arrives at my table, he leans over and speaks in a conspiratorial whisper that, of course, everyone within four square miles can hear. "The purpose of the clay lies here," he says, pointing to my head, "and here," my heart this time, "and here," he touches my hands as if they are prized jewels.

"It is in the head, the heart, the hands of its master. It is there that a shapeless lump of earth achieves greatness or functionality or even disuse. What is the purpose of your lump of clay? Only to bend its very life to the will of its master and by doing so, to fulfill its eternal destiny. Or at least until your mom throws it out in the garbage two months from now." He grins at our laughter. He has won us over, and he knows it. Now it is time to create.

I sit for a while, reading the lines on the block in front of me. It is mine to shape, to carve, to strengthen, and to crumble. I reach to its middle, intending to bend the edges toward me, and find it won't budge. I am surprised, and apply more force, only to see an ugly scar appear in a place I had not anticipated.

"Mr. Houlihan!" I call out. "My clay is defective. I need another piece."

Mr. H comes quickly to my side, holding a bowl of water and a sponge. "No, Todd. It's just resisting your will. But it can learn. With a gentle touch and a little moisture, you'll find it quite open to living out your purpose."

I regard him with perspective of a 12-year-old know-it-all. "You talk like this stuff is alive."

He smiles. "Aah, but isn't it, almost? All it lacks is the breath of life from a creator, and it can come to life in ways we can't imagine. Michelangelo, Da Vinci, they could all breath life into a work of art." He peers into my eyes. "Yes, I see that spark of divine creativity in you, Todd. You, too, can give the gift of life, can create art out of this worthless lump of clay. You can give it a purpose beyond its wildest dreams."

"You're crazy, Mr. H, you know that don't you?"

He laughs, a hearty, pleasant laugh. "Yes, I guess I am a little crazy," he says with a wink. "But so are you." He claps me on the shoulder and moves to help Shawna Kyle.

I begin drizzling water from the sponge over the edges of my clay. At first it seems to be crying, then the moisture is soaked into the material and with gentle exercise it begins to loosen and soften. When I finally spread it out flat on my desk I feel a thrill and the rest of the classroom seems to fade away.

"What will you be?" I say to myself, to the clay. "Will you follow my designs for you now?"

It responds in my hands, and by the end of the class I've completed two-thirds of a miniature tiger. It isn't perfect, no, but all who look at it can at least tell what it's going to be, and that gives me a sense of accomplishment. My mind is already racing with ideas about how to paint and preserve my little lump of clay.

"When can we finish our artwork, Mr. Houlihan?" I ask on my way out.

"Todd," he says with a knowing hand on my shoulder, "a work of art is never finished. Its purpose, its existence, its goals are constantly being refined by its creator."

I nod and leave. This, at least, is something I understand.

• • •

We Talk about Pain

IT'S DIFFICULT, I THINK, to have a big secret and not share it with somebody. Even if that secret is proof that you might be certifiably insane, something within demands that your secret be told. That's why I made the call. At least that's why I told myself I was making the call.

The phone cycled through five rings before her answering machine picked up. "Hey, we can't come to the phone right now, so leave a message after the beep and we'll call you back. Have a great day!"

Just hearing her voice made my heart race again. I felt like I was that anxious guy who had called her up several years ago to request a first date. *Silly*, I thought. *No reason to be nervous.*

"Beeep."

"Hey, uh, Nat. It's Todd. Listen, I just wanted to call and see how you were doing and stuff. Also, you know, I met somebody recently, and I thought you might really like to meet him too. Anyway, I'm going over to visit him this afternoon and just wanted to—"

"Hello, Todd."

I groaned inwardly. "Oh, hey Doug. How's it going?"

I could hear Doug Green sighing into the telephone. "Listen, Todd, I don't mean to be rude, but don't you think you're out of line calling here now?"

"Doug, I—"

"I mean, I know you and Natalie had a good thing going for a long time. But I gotta' be honest with you, man. You messed it up, and now Nat and I have a good thing going. I can't let you mess that up too. You know?"

"Doug, I'm not trying to steal your wife away from you. I—"

"That's right. You're NOT. That's why I'm asking you not to call here anymore."

"You don't understand. I'm happy for you and Natalie. I really am. I hope you live happily ever after and have dozens of kids and stuff. But Nat and I are—were at least—very good friends. I just want to be friends with her still. And I met somebody I think she'd—"

"Don't do this to yourself, Todd, or to Natalie, or to me. I mean, we've only been married nine months, and you're already calling to ask her out on a date? Show some respect, man. If not for her, at least for yourself."

"I'm not—"

"I'm hanging up now, Todd. And right after that, I'm erasing your message. Maybe someday—five, ten years down the road—you and Nat can rekindle your friendship without all that emotional baggage that comes with having been once engaged. But right now, she's happy, man. And we're going to get on with our lives. You need to do the same."

"Doug, you've got me it wrong. I—"

"Goodbye, Todd."

It was stupid, I know, to call her again. All it did was remind me of the loneliness I'd worked hard to forget—and of how stupid I was in general.

I had planned to go down to Newport Beach that day, to look for moments. In the back of my mind I was toying with the idea of a book of ocean photography and was hoping to pull in a few images that would be good for that kind of project. Instead (after I contemplated chucking my telephone into traffic) I just sat on my couch, breathing hard, swearing just a bit and, much to my surprise, trying not to cry.

I took control after only a few moments, but the ache in my insides took longer to go away. I found myself staring at the paint on my walls and wondering where I could get some of that sunlight paint that Jackson put all over Matthew's apartment.

Finally I gave up and opened an old closet I'd kept closed for the last eighteen months or so. Inside it smelled like musty paper and dusty clothes. The little box on the shelf above made me smile grudgingly.

"At least she had the decency to return my ring," I muttered.

Lined up next to that little box was a row of shoeboxes, each carefully arranged and covered. I took down two of them and returned to the living room.

Reading through the notes and love letters and scraps of souvenirs from countless dates together made me feel a little better in a miserable sort of way. Burning them in my sink brought back that feeling of inexplicable loss that I'd tried so hard to forget.

When I'd washed the flaking remains of charred paper down the garbage disposal, I picked up the second shoebox and decided to take it with me to visit Matthew.

"Greetings, friend Todd!" He made a hand gesture my way, then extended for my grip. "You're early, but that makes for a better day in my way of thinking."

It was dripping hot outside, and I was grateful when Calia inserted a tall glass of iced Mountain Dew into my hand. Inside was stuffy and warm too, but Jackson left the front door and windows open, and apparently had been airing out the apartment all day. Two fans in opposite corners of the living room whirred their defiance at the heat, and a ceiling fan spun overhead in the dining/kitchen area.

For his part, Matthew looked as comfortable in the heat as a dog in the shade, and was wearing surf pants and a tank-top under-shirt. My Disney cap was perched happily—if not perfectly—atop his head. I was surprised to see that, while he was solid, there didn't seem to be an ounce of flab on the man. I guess death had been good for him, physically.

"You'd think a prophet and two angels could afford a window air conditioner or something."

He cocked his head and listened intently while Calia explained what a window air conditioner was.

"Sounds like a wonderful tool, Todd," he laughed. "But this is more like what I was used to before."

I nodded, trying not to sweat into my drink. He looked at me with piercing eyes, and involuntarily I looked away. "So, what do you do the rest of the week when I'm not here?"

He patted me on the shoulder. "That," he said, "is irrelevant. What matters is that I see a new sorrow in your eyes today, Todd. Or perhaps it's an old one I never noticed before?"

"Don't waste any time, do you?"

"Time is something that is also irrelevant. Especially to a man who has been both dead and alive, right?"

I didn't say anything and instead took in the miraculous paint on the walls. The tint had changed—it had been imbued with a sunburst orange that now seemed to radiate within the walls themselves.

"Jackson is an angel of many talents, isn't he?" Matthew smiled.

The angel in question interrupted our tête-à-tête just

then, appearing from out of nowhere, as he often seemed to do. Standing in the open doorway he said casually, "You all feel like getting out of this stuffy apartment?"

Calia stood. "Excuse me a minute, Todd." She took Jackson by the arm and stepped outside where they held a whispered conference. Matthew looked at me with eyebrows raised in question. Apparently this wasn't an interruption he expected.

Calia reentered the apartment smiling. "Todd, how about if we bring along that shoebox and expose Matthew to the delights of freshly-picked strawberries? Jackson tells me there's a roadside stand over in Fullerton that allows buyers to actually go into their patch and pick berries straight off the vines. Whaddya say? My treat." She flashed a few bills and rattled her keys to the Toyota.

I started to object. Something seemed fishy here. But Matthew put a hand on my shoulder, waiting. And to be honest, fresh, sweet, juicy strawberries did sound pretty good at the moment. I shrugged. "Sure," I said. "Sounds great."

As we turned the corner to go down the steps of the apartment building, I heard a loud rapping. I peeked back just in time to see Jackson standing in front of Miranda's door. Calia tapped my arm.

"Don't worry," she said softly. "Jackson'll take care of Miranda."

"What are you talking about?" I said.

She just laughed. "I know you better than you think I do, Todd. So does Jackson. And that's why he's going to invite Miranda out for an ice cream cone. So don't worry. She'll be fine. Now c'mon. I haven't had fresh strawberries in ages!"

She bounced down the stairs, catching up with Matthew at the bottom. And I realized that our hasty exit from the Breezewood Arms did make me a little uneasy for the next-door neighbor, though I couldn't for the life of me figure out why.

I heard the door to apartment 24 open in the background as I followed the Apostle and the angel to Calia's red Toyota Camry. Before long we were heading down Orangethorpe toward the city of Fullerton. Of course, the "cities" in this stretch of southern California are really indistinguishable from each other—lots of concrete, shopping malls, and housing districts all smashed together for miles and miles and miles. But the city borders are important to those of us who live here, and my mind automatically kept track of the fact that we'd have to leave Whittier and go through La Mirada on our way to the strawberry patch.

Just before we entered La Mirada, the sound of sirens reached my ears. It grew louder for a few moments, then seemed to fade as we drove further away from the Breezewood Arms. I chanced a look at Calia, saw her checking the rearview mirror for a moment, then she seemed to relax and settle into the routine of driving.

"So what's in the box, friend Todd?" The Apostle sat in the back seat, taking the position that Calia had occupied during my first car ride with the angels. He and she had both insisted that I take the front passenger seat. I had set the box of photographs on the seat next to me, between my chair and Calia's driver seat.

I sighed.

"Pain," I said. "That's what's in the box. Guess I'm feeling like a glutton for punishment today."

Matthew nodded. "Care to show it to me?"

"Not really. No, that's not true. I do want to show it to you, or I wouldn't have brought it along, right? It's just, now that we're here, I don't care to look at it again myself."

"How about if I help myself, then?"

"Knock yourself out."

He gave me a puzzled look.

"I mean, sure. Go ahead."

Matthew reached over the seat and removed the lid from my box, extracting a handful of photos from the opened top.

"She's lovely," he said.

"Which picture are you looking at?"

"It appears to be an attractive young woman, sitting in your lap at a party. You both look quite happy."

I closed my eyes, remembering my 31st birthday and the way she looked.

"Yes," I said. Let's see. "If I remember correctly, she has her hair up in a clip, bunched just a bit to the side on the left. You can't tell it from the picture, but she had really long hair then. Straight, black, and falling midway down her back. She's wearing a summer dress—blue with red rose prints. Her skin is the color of a caramel apple, rich and sugary, with just a tint of red under the surface. Deep brown eyes. And a body that felt like it weighed nothing whenever she was in my arms."

Matthew patted my shoulder. "I begin to see. What's her name?"

"Natalie Kordai. Or just Nat to her friends. I was her friend once."

"More than a friend?"

"Yeah."

"And now?"

"Now she is a 'friend' to someone else."

I choked. With an unexpected swiftness a wracking sob spilled out of my mouth, and the headache that had been threatening released itself in my temples while the tears began to flow. I felt the sting of disappointment piercing my gut—and felt embarrassed at how ludicrous I must have appeared at that moment. I turned my head toward the window to avoid looking at Matthew—or at Calia, for that matter—and somehow caught my breath in such a way that the tightness of my chest squeezed air out instead of in. Now I had both the embarrassment of crying like a baby and the pain of getting the wind knocked out of me at the same time.

To their credit, both Matthew and Calia simply waited, saying nothing. Finally, thankfully, I was able to sweep in a lung full of air and hold it, willing my eyes to dry and increasing the tension in my head at the same time. I wiped my face on my sleeve.

"Sorry," I said. "Didn't expect to do that. Guess I must have cared about her more than I wanted to admit."

Matthew nodded. He looked through the next few photos in his stack before returning them to the box.

"She is lovely," he said. "I can see it in her eyes. She has the spark of the Creator burning brightly within."

"Yeah. We were engaged to be married once. But I messed that up. Now she's married to someone else, and I have lost the best friend I ever knew."

We sat in silence a moment while I collected myself. In a minute or two, I felt almost normal again, except for a splitting headache—and an eternal emptiness inside.

"This life hurts, Matthew—a lot."

"I know."

"Why does it have to? Not just for me. For everybody. For people who are ill, or victims of war or crime, or abandonment, or hunger. There's no end to the ways we cause each other pain. Why does God allow us to suffer? Why is sorrow always so close to happiness? Why does life always inflict pain right alongside its joys?"

"We're here." Calia parked the Toyota in a dirt lot alongside a strawberry patch at the corner of Orangethorpe and Bastanchury. She gave me an apologetic look. "Sorry to interrupt. But why don't you and Matthew continue the conversation while we're picking berries?"

We got out and joined the small crowd of customers. There were more people than I'd realistically expected for a stinky-hot Tuesday afternoon. But the folks at the stand were cheery and passing out ice water along with little plastic green strawberry baskets, and everyone seemed to appreciate it.

Matthew and I hung back while Calia went up and paid for our baskets. She returned with these instructions: "The lady said we can fill these baskets up to the top with anything we pick, and that after we can sit under that shade tree to eat them if we want." She pointed to the northeast corner of the lot. "The only thing is, she said that area back in that corner is off limits unless we like weeds."

Calia distributed our baskets and we walked out into the garden patch to begin picking. Matthew hadn't spoken since we got out of the car, and now his face still held a serious, contemplative look. After a moment, he touched Calia's shoulder and said something in Aramaic. The angel didn't seem to be interpreting, so I assumed he was asking her a question. She cocked her head in response, apparently considering some suggestion. Next she excused herself from us and went back to the attendant at the roadside booth. When she returned, she spoke a few words at Matthew. He nodded thoughtfully, asked her another question. She responded with some kind of explanation. Then she put an arm around his shoulders and mine, and steered us directly to the "off limits" corner of the patch.

"What's this all about?" I asked.

"I think," Matthew said, "that this may be a better place for us to choose our berries. So I asked Calia if she would secure permission for us to pick here."

We strode into the middle of the weedy segment, and I saw that Matthew was right. Hidden amidst the plants were thick, red bunches of strawberries. Many a plump berry was ready to be pulled from the vine, but there were also a number of plants still in the ripening phase of growth. And there were dandelions everywhere, wrapped in and out of some plants, growing tall above others, some yellow in bloom, others white and flicking little dandelion seeds across this corner of the strawberry patch.

"Well, Matthew, there certainly are berries mixed in here. But there are also quite a few dandelion weeds mixed in."

I pointed to a plant nearby.

"Look at this one," I said. "We can't pick the berries without picking a dandelion or two along with them. It would have been better if these farmers had cleared the weeds out of here first."

"Look more closely at that plant," Matthew said. "What do you think would happen if someone tried to rip out that dandelion?"

I kneeled down to get a better peek at the plant in question. The dandelion had apparently seeded right next to the roots of the strawberry plant because two yellow shoots poked through the center of the berry bunches, making the weed essentially inseparable from the fruit of the plant.

"You can't," I said finally. "If you pull out that weed you will kill the plant. They'll have to wait until the harvest is over, then pull out both and then replant good seed without weeds in it."

"But don't you think that weed is hurting the plant? Wouldn't it be better to end its suffering now?"

"Well, yeah, the weed is stealing water and nutrients from the strawberry plant. But if you pull it out before the fruit is fully ripened then you've killed off the plant for nothing. Better to wait it out, I think. At least then something good will come alongside the bad."

"You know a lot about plants and weeds, Todd."

"Not really. It's just basic gardening sense."

"And you know a lot about life, whether you realize it or not."

"What do you mean?"

"I mean, I believe you've just answered your own question this week."

"How could I have done that? We haven't even been talking about my question."

"Haven't we? You asked why God would allow pain to be such a part of a person's life."

"Yes?"

"Todd, Calia asked the attendant over there how this section of her garden came to be infested with weeds. Turns out one of her employees did it. He found out he was being paid less than another worker. Didn't think it was fair. So one Friday during work, he pretended to be fertilizing and nurturing the plants in this corner. But in reality he was mixing dandelion seeds into the fertilizer he spread on each plant, turning the earth to help it sink it with the strawberries. Monday morning, he skipped out of town. They haven't seen him again. But after the plants started growing they discovered his evil plan. The weeds he'd planted were growing right alongside the good plants, choking out some and simply being a nuisance to others.

"The owner of this plot decided the same thing you did. If they dug out the weeds, it would kill all the plants over here. So instead they decided to let the berries grow in the middle of this dandelion infestation. At the end of the harvest, they will rescue all the good fruit before tearing out the weeds once and for all."

"That's all very interesting. But I still don't see what it

has to do with my question."

"Todd, you and I are the good fruit. God has planted us here to grow and thrive. The enemy, however, has planted weeds in God's garden, and those 'dandelions' cause us pain. Should God root out those weeds and destroy us along with them? No, friend Todd. He's willing to let us suffer in order that we might live."

He reached down and pulled a plump berry from a vine nearby. "And even in this hardship, by the great Gardener's grace, some will still overcome and thrive."

I paused to look at Matthew. There he stood, looking both young and innocent, and old and wise.

"You're a pretty smart guy, Matthew."

He shook his head modestly. "Actually, I'm not," he said. "I'm just adapting for you a story that Jesus once told to me. He's the smart one."

"Life still hurts, Matthew. Still hurts a lot."

"I know, Todd. But the pain doesn't have to kill you." He looked meaningfully into my eyes. "Don't let it kill you, Todd."

In spite of all the weeds in that corner, it took us only about fifteen minutes to fill our baskets full of ripe, red strawberries. And only about five minutes more to polish them off under the shade tree on the lot. Afterward, my hands and lips felt sticky, and there were red juice stains around the corner of Matthew's mouth. But for some reason, the tension behind my temples had eased a bit, and I was grateful.

The car ride back to Matthew's apartment was a quiet one. A cool breeze had begun to pick up as sunset neared, and we all luxuriated in the wind flying through the windows of Calia's Camry.

Jackson met us at the curb outside the Breezewood

Arms. "I see you had success," he said as he opened my car door. Before I could respond, Miranda appeared at the bottom of the steps.

"Everything's pretty much cleaned up in there now, Jack," she said. "All I can say is it's a good thing you stopped by when you did! Just think what might have happened if I'd been inside there when that outlet blew! As it is, it looks like I'm going to have to get a new stove, but the firefighters got here so fast they were able to stop the fire before it had a chance to do much damage."

She stopped short, noticing the rest of us for the first time. "Well, hello there. Guy with the loud knock, right?" She gave a wearied smile.

"Um, yes. My name's Todd. Sorry to hear about your apartment."

She looked backward toward the stairs. "Well, I guess you have to take the bad with the good in this life."

"I'm learning that, too," I said.

"Anyway, I'm just glad somebody up there was looking out for me today." She reached out and squeezed Jackson's muscled arm. "Thanks for the ice cream, Jack. I'll see you again soon."

Miranda disappeared up the steps while I looked at Jackson with renewed curiosity. He avoided my gaze and instead walked down the sidewalk a bit, as if he were taking up a bodyguard position for Matthew.

"Thanks for going to get strawberries with me, Todd," Matthew said. "They were a delicious treat."

"Yes, they were. And thank you, Matthew."

"See you next week, then?" He extended his hand for a shake.

"Wouldn't miss it," I said. Then an idea hit me.

"How do you feel about fishing?"

• • •

I am crying.

I am crying.

I feel the pain of my tears in every pore of my skin, an acid that burns me from within.

Her words echo still within my skull. Did I really do this? Did I really let my fears drive her away?

"I love you, Todd," she had said. "Enough to let you go."

"I think I love you, Nat. It's just ..."

How could I have been so stupid to say that? To do what I did?

"No, Todd. Don't say anymore. This hurts too much already."

Which is worse, I wonder, that I hurt so badly, or that I caused her to hurt even worse?

"I'll notify the guests that you've—we've—canceled the wedding, Todd. My parents will—" her voice catches then, but her eyes refuse to let the tears well up. "My parents will help me. We'll take care of it all, Todd. You just go take care of yourself."

I remember that I finished that sentence in my head when she said it. "Take care of yourself, Todd. That's what you're good at anyway."

She left, then. Two weeks before the wedding date. We haven't talked since. And now it is the day my marriage was to begin, the night that "happily ever after" was to become the description of my life.

What have I done?

Why is it that only now I realize I need Natalie more than I need breath or food or light? Why must pain be the tool that clarifies my heart's longings? Why couldn't our happy times have done that for me two weeks ago?

She is gone now. For good. I heard she left California for a while. No one will tell me where she is, not even my friends. "You've caused her enough pain already, Todd," they say. "Give her some time to heal before you mess with her heart again, OK buddy?"

I lay on the floor of my condominium now, feeling the blinding power of self-inflicted loneliness.

Oh, Nat. I'm so sorry. I was a fool.

I am crying. I am crying.

It feels as though I will never stop.

• • •

We Talk about Wealth

JACKSON WAS ALREADY THERE when I walked up the Balboa Pier at Newport Beach. He was standing behind Ruby's Diner, leaning back against the railing with a newspaper folded and tucked under his arm. The sky was too dark for reading yet, but in the distance dull streaks of light suggested dawn was on its way, preparing to light up a brand new day.

I considered asking Jackson to help me carry the fishing equipment—two rods, a bucket, and a tackle box filled with chunks of bait and hooks and lures and anything else I could think to cram in there. But, for some reason, what he was doing—just standing there watching my progress up the pier—seemed more important than helping me carry my load. He nodded my direction, but didn't speak.

Although sinfully early by my standards, I wasn't surprised to see a few other hopeful fishermen dotting the edge of the pier. We all appeared to have dressed from the same catalog. Even though the summer day would heat up soon enough, the combination of a cool wind off the ocean and the early-morning temperatures necessitated long pants (jeans in most cases) and either a sweatshirt or light jacket over a tee. As the morning evolved, most of us would dump the jacket/sweatshirt and roll up our pant legs to cool off before finally heading home around midday, when the beach would fill with noisy tourists and sun-seeking locals. Down the coast a bit, small groups of surfers had already staked out their spots in the sand, riding the chilly waves in wetsuits and drinking in more saltwater in a day than the rest of us would swallow in a year.

A light was on inside Ruby's, and as I walked by I caught sight of a solitary worker already preparing the 1940s diner to greet the customers of the day. Soon a few other employees would join him, and together they'd begin serving coffee and eggs to the patrons at the beach and pier. By noontime they'd be packed with visitors clamoring to sit in the red vinyl booths hungry for burgers and malts, hot dogs and sodas, and spilling ketchup and mustard all over the spotless white Formica-and-chrome tables lined up inside.

But for now at least, the pier was near-silent. A rugged-looking fisherman—an older gentleman—had taken one corner at the end of the dock, quietly smoking a cigarette, lost in his thoughts and waiting for a bite. Down a bit from him stood a dad and a boy of about 10. The dad was teaching the youngster how to cast a line, but their voices were soft and easily drowned by the rolling waves. On the other side a middle-aged woman and man leaned over the edge of the pier, arm-in-arm, huddled close for warmth and operating a single fishing pole between them.

All that was left on the Balboa Pier that morning was me, feeling a little chilled, a little nervous, and wondering why I'd ever suggested to Matthew that we do anything that occurred in pre-dawn hours. I set up my gear in the corner across from the old fisherman. I figured he looked most like he knew where the fish would be thick and hoped to catch a few that got away from him. Jackson stayed where he was, back by the diner, looking like an undercover sentry trying to blend in but failing to do so completely. I threaded the two fishing poles, one for me and one for Matthew, and then worried that I probably should have brought an extra in case Calia or Jackson had wanted to fling a line or two. Then I waited, wishing that Ruby's would hurry up and open so I could start filling my insides with a warm liquid while I waited.

I did a double take when Matthew appeared at the end of the pier. Calia was with him, looking every bit the Southern California beauty in a bright blue sundress covered over in a waist-length jacket and a stylish straw hat. Matthew, on the other hand, looked ... well, to be honest he looked ridiculous.

She and Matthew were obviously chatting about something and laughing with each step they took. The old man across from me glanced back at the Apostle and snorted before raising his eyebrows my direction. I mustered a half-smile and the "must be a tourist" shrug that we Californians have perfected over the years. Then I swallowed my pride and walked back his direction to meet him.

"Greetings, friend Todd! What a lovely morning this is. I can practically taste the salt in the air, and that—" he pointed toward the east, "is a superb sunrise brewing, I can tell." Matthew extended his hand my direction, and we shook.

"Nice suit," I said. "What is that, a double-breasted linen outfit?"

He smiled approvingly and nodded, taking a moment to model the ensemble for me.

"Matthew, it looks great on you. That kind of pale green material has a very rich look to it, and the gold-striped tie is definitely a nice touch. But, well, it's not exactly a *fishing* outfit, is it?"

He laughed, a hearty, friendly laugh that I now conjure up in my imagination whenever I'm feeling happy. "She told me you'd say that," he nodded toward Calia. "But it doesn't matter. It's not what the fisherman *wears,* but what he *does* that counts." He clapped me on the shoulder. "Have you got a place for us?"

I pointed toward the end of the pier and Matthew went whistling toward my gear. As he walked ahead, I noticed that he'd worn his old, beat-up sandals instead of dress shoes.

"Toes must be freezing," I muttered to myself. But he seemed completely comfortable, so I decided to let it drop.

"Now, fishing in my day was something a bit different than it is today, I understand," Matthew said. He picked up a rod and began examining the reel, tracing the fishing line through the loops on the pole to the hook that dangled from its end. "Where I come from, fishermen made extensive use of nets for their task. My friends used to weight down the bottom edge of a cast net, then with great skill throw it into the water so that it would fan out and sink to the sea floor. Next they'd dive in the water, gather the weights together to close up the net, and drag it back to the surface. If all went as planned, a load of fish that could be eaten or sold was caught in the net. It was hard work and took a measure of skill and patience that many didn't have. But it wasn't without its rewards, either."

"People still do that in some parts of the world. But amateurs like the rest of us usually just throw a line into the water and hope a fish bites so we can reel it in."

We spent a few moments going over the mechanisms of our fishing poles and practicing how to flick our bait over the edge and into the ocean (without impaling anyone nearby with the hooks). Matthew was a quick learner, and before long he settled into his corner of the pier as comfortably as the grizzled old veteran across the dock from us.

The sun soon peeked in earnest over the edge of the horizon and, almost involuntarily, those of us on the pier diverted our attention to the show in the sky. The blazing yellow fired up the morning, its warmth hinting at the stifling heat yet to come. But for now at least, the strength of that heat was still tempered by the cool ocean breeze and the early morning fog.

"You know," Matthew sighed, "if the sun rose only once in a decade, we would consider ourselves rich men to see that sight just a few times before we died. As it is, we see it thousands of times and forget the wealth God has packed into those few precious moments each day."

Matthew pushed up the sleeves on his suit coat and returned his attention to trolling his fishing line in the water below. I flung my line out to the west of his, hoping that between the two of us we'd pull in something.

On the beach to our right newcomers started to appear: a few more surfers, a girl with a book, and of course a man with a metal detector.

Mr. Metal Detector took a few minutes to set up his equipment, then he began a long, slow crawl along the shoreline, waving his machinery in a practiced motion across the sand in front of each step. I watched him with mild curiosity, wondering at the patience behind his task and curious why he chose to do this to seek his fortune rather than applying his obvious determination to a more fruitful career.

He walked along for a good stretch of beach before finally finding something worth stopping for. He carefully laid aside his tool and quickly pulled from his back pocket a spade, which he subsequently applied to the sand. After a time of digging, he pulled something out of the ground and gave it a quick examination. Even from this distance, I could tell his face wore a mask of disgust as he tossed the item out toward the waves. He picked up the metal detector and continued his solitary work.

"You've got a bite."

"What? Oh! Thanks, Matthew. Almost missed it."

I started to reel in a fish, but almost as quickly as I began winding the line, it went slack in my hands. Went I pulled up the hook my suspicions were confirmed.

"Stole your bait, did he?" Matthew smiled and patted my arm.

"Yeah. Maybe you'll get him instead."

"Maybe."

We fell silent while I re-baited my hook and then cast it into the water below. Then Matthew nodded toward Mr. Metal Detector down on the beach.

"That man," he said. "What's he doing?"

"Looking for buried treasure."

"What treasure will he find here?"

I chanced another look down at our wealth-seeking friend before responding.

"He's hoping to find valuables that others may have lost and left behind in the sand on the beach," I said. "Coins. Gold rings. Jewelry. That kind of thing. His metal detector can scan for metal objects, and it starts beeping when it locates something metal in the ground. That's when he stops to dig and see what he will find."

Matthew nodded. "Will he find wealth this way?"

"Probably not. But everybody wants riches, and this is the way he's figured out to make his, I guess."

"Seems like a lot of effort for little gain."

"Better that than what some others do. Lie. Steal, Murder. Cheat. Intimidate. Bully. Pretty much anything it takes to gain another—"

I realized suddenly that the person I was describing could easily have been a tax collector two thousand years ago.

"Matthew, um, I'm sorry. I didn't mean—you know."

He smiled and re-cast his line. "No need to apologize, Todd. I know who I was, and I know who I am now thanks to the grace of Christ. And you are right. People will do almost anything for the empty promise of wealth."

"Why is that, Matthew? Why are we so obsessed with riches in this world?"

"Aah, so we finally get to the question today."

I chuckled. "Yes, I guess so," I said. "No, wait. Let me rephrase the question. Humanity has been obsessed with riches for all of history, but most often those who manage to acquire it live out their days in unhappiness anyway. So I guess my question is, what is true wealth anyway? What is it exactly that we're so desperate to acquire?"

"Well, if it's success at fishing, I'm an impoverished man!" Matthew laid aside his pole and turned his face toward the ever-brightening sun. He pushed up the sleeves on his suit coat, and I followed his lead, letting my jacket drape over the side of the pier. After a moment he looked back at Mr. Metal Detector.

"I heard a story once, Todd. It seems there was a man out wandering through a deserted field. He paused to rest under a large shade tree, and while sitting there he noticed an odd accumulation of rocks stacked nearby. It was almost as if the rocks were there to mark something.

"The man went to investigate. Under the pile of rocks he found a small shovel. 'Curious!' he thought. The earth beneath the rocks looked just like any other in this field, but it appeared to hold a secret begging to be discovered. The man spent the next several hours digging, growing increasingly excited and curious. Just under the surface someone had buried a sizeable wooden box. He dug around the edges until he had freed up access to the lid on the box. With the bulk of the box still in the ground, he lifted off the lid and was astounded by what he saw.

"Glittering inside the box was a hidden treasure. It was a fortune—more than he could ever imagine!

"The man sat staring at the riches before him for awhile, then he made a decision. Carefully resealing the lid on the box, he worked into the night packing dirt over the treasure once more, concealing the wealth back in the ground where he had found it.

"The next morning, he immediately sought out the owner of the field and asked to purchase it. The price for the land was high—more than the man had expected. In fact, it would cost everything the man owned: his home, his furniture, his livestock—even the very clothes in his wardrobe. But he didn't hesitate. He went out and sold all that he had, save the clothes on his back, to raise enough money to buy the field. When he had it all, he happily traded it all for the right to own the treasure buried in a barren field."

"Must have been some treasure. What was in the box?"

Matthew shrugged. "What would you have in the box?"

"What?"

"The real treasure wasn't in the contents of the box. It was in the desires of the man's heart … in the fact that this man was willing—no, desperate—to give anything and everything he had to make this treasure his own."

"Tell me—what kind of treasure is worth all that?"

Matthew stood up straight, flattening out the creases in his expensive suit. "Would clothes like this be enough?"

I shook my head.

"How about this?" He reached into a pocket and pulled out a fat wad of American money. It appeared to be all one hundred dollar bills.

"Where did you get that? And don't hold it out in the open like that. You never know who might—"

"It doesn't matter, Todd. This isn't a treasure in my

heart. Is it in yours?"

"It's sure tempting."

"But is it worth everything you have?"

I shook my head slowly. I knew money could never buy happiness. Nothing real, anyway.

Matthew held the wad of cash over the edge of the pier. I could see the eyes of the old fisherman across from us widen at the Apostle's actions. Matthew then rubbed his fingers together, letting hundred dollar bills float carelessly out into the wind and drop to the water below. The old fisherman started to pack up his gear in a hurry. Then he saw the middle-aged couple staring and pointing at Matthew. They all dropped their fishing equipment and raced down toward the end of the dock, apparently intent on retrieving some of Matthew's irrelevant treasure.

"So what is it, Todd? When all is said and done, what really is worth everything you are and everything you own?"

"I guess I don't know yet, Matthew."

"Think about it, then."

So I did. In a couple of minutes I saw the middle-aged woman diving into the water below, swimming around in search for hundred dollar bills. She was soon joined by the old fisherman, and the dad and son. Down the beach I saw a surfer point. They'd be here before long too.

"Looks like our fishing is over," I said, motioning to the commotion below.

Matthew nodded noncommittally. "Looks like."

I watched the treasure-seekers, and after a moment it sunk in. These folks would go home happy today, a few hundred—maybe a few thousand—dollars richer. But sooner or later, their newfound riches would be gone. Sooner or later they'd have to go treasure hunting again— looking for money or new jobs or ways to pay bills or to increase their security.

Matthew interrupted my thoughts. "I met a man once who had it all. He was a rich man, his coffers filled with gold. His household was large enough to require—and afford—a number of servants to care for it. Fancy tapestries, expensive rugs inside. The best food each night on his table. Wore a ring of gold and a necklace of braided silver.

"He was also a religious man. Honorable, upright. Concerned with honesty and matters of the law. Well-respected by all."

"He was wealthy, then?"

"No. He was rich, but not wealthy. He had acquired a lot, but all he had was only temporary. So he went looking for eternity.

"He ended up at Jesus. 'Teacher,' he asked 'what good thing must I do to get eternal life?' Jesus told him the standard answer. 'Obey the commandments.' But something within this young man needed more than that. He was looking for the unimaginable wealth of heaven, and he knew Jesus was the One who could help him find it.

"'All these I have kept,' he said. 'What do I still lack?'

"And in one hand, Jesus held out to him that which he so desperately craved—treasure that can't rust, riches that will never fade. In the other hand, Christ held out the cost: everything.

"'Go, sell your possessions and give to the poor ... Then come, follow me.'"

"I watched him, then. We all did, waiting to see how this rich man would respond. Did he see what we saw? Did he understand the wealth that was being offered to him? I suspect his stomach growled then, but he put a hand there as if to acknowledge his hunger. He absentmindedly fingered the braided silver around his neck. He glanced over at one of the servants who had accompanied him to meet with Jesus. And it finally sunk in. Jesus was asking for it all. The eternal treasure Christ offered would cost him everything in his temporary life."

"So what did he do?"

Matthew looked at me with a level gaze that didn't flinch. "Same thing you did."

He waited then, never loosing his eyes from mine. I nodded and looked away. I didn't need Matthew to finish the story for me. I knew how it ended. The rich young man turned and ran.

"Yeah, well," I said. "At least I'm stopping for a breather for the moment."

He put a hand on my shoulder, a gesture that I realized reminded me of my father. "True wealth, Todd," he said, "lasts forever. It is never temporary like money or comforts or even relationships that end in death. True wealth never fades; it is always enough."

"You speak as if you know this from experience.

"Oh I do, Todd. I do."

"Anybody interested in coffee and pancakes?" Jackson had finally brought himself into our little company. "Ruby's Diner is open now."

Matthew smiled and nodded, and Calia said, "Sounds good to me. How about you Todd? Want to continue your conversation indoors?"

Moments later we were all transported back to the 1940s in a red vinyl booth inside Ruby's. Outside a growing crowd had gathered on the pier, scouring the corners and cracks looking for hidden cash that might have gotten caught there.

"So, Todd," Matthew said between forkfuls of a syrup-drenched breakfast. "Shall we meet back at the apartment next week?"

• • •

"Two-fifty is my bid, do I hear three? Three? Three hundred

dollars for this fine piece?"

Natalie and I sit in the art auction, bored. We've been dating seriously now for just over a year. When I told her I had a few photos set to sell in this auction—a first for me—she insisted on coming along. Now I fear she regrets her decision to join me.

"Why would anybody pay that much for an imitation of a Van Gogh painting?" she asks. "I mean, you can buy a print for twenty bucks at most any poster store."

I nod. She's right. Although the artist here apparently went to great lengths to imitate Vincent Van Gogh's original, in the end it's still just a copycat.

"Three hundred from the woman in the yellow hat. Anybody bid three-fifty? Three-and-a-quarter?"

"How much longer before they get to your photographs, Todd? My behind is starting to get sore from this metal chair."

I check the lot listing. "It looks like I'm next. But this one seems to be dragging on. Want to take a walk or something while we wait?"

"Three-twenty-five from the gentleman in black. Do I hear three-fifty?"

Nat sighs. "Nah, I guess I can wait it out. Who's that?"

She points to a representative of the auction house now making his way up to the auctioneer.

"Three-fifty from the lady in the yellow hat. Do I hear—excuse me a moment."

The auction house rep and the auctioneer huddle in conference. From where I sit, I see the auctioneer's eyebrows raise. He's put a hand over the microphone, but we can still make out snatches of his conversation.

"Why wasn't I told this before ... can't stop now ... can you be sure ... fine ... take care of it."

The rep steps gingerly to the display and much to our surprise, removes the painting from the display area.

"Well, friends," the auctioneer says, "it appears there's going to be a little excitement here today after all. This item has been unexpectedly removed from the auction block by its owner pending further research into its authorship."

"What's that supposed to mean, Harry?" shouts a voice from somewhere on the floor.

The auctioneer steals a quick glance at the auction rep, who simply shrugs. "Well, Mr. Logan," he finally responds, "the owner of this piece owns the original Van Gogh. She liked it so much she commissioned the copycat artwork. Trouble is, she now can't tell the two canvases apart. At the last minute she asked to have this one removed from today's sale so she can have an expert determine which is the real treasure—and thus much more valuable than $350—and which is the imitation."

A tittering of laughter sprinkles through the audience.

Natalie's jaw drops. "Does that mean somebody almost bought an original Van Gogh for only $350? Wow. Talk about a hidden treasure, huh?"

I chuckle. "I guess if you're gonna get rich in this business, you gotta' know the difference between real wealth and cheap imitations."

Nat gives me a funny look, as if she's considering something. "You know, Todd," she says finally. "I think that's the smartest thing you've said in a long time."

I shrug, unimpressed. "Great. Now hush up. This next piece is one of mine ..."

• • •

The Seventh Tuesday

We Talk about Faith

THE FIRST TUESDAY in August a miracle happened: it rained. Rain seems like a rare thing in SoCal anyway, and for it to appear in late summer is almost unheard of. But there it was, unmistakably drizzling down from the skies.

It was lunchtime when I first noticed. I'd spent the morning back at the SuperSol toy company, finishing the shoot that had been so rudely interrupted several weeks before. Everything went without a hitch this time, and even traffic was manageable enough to allow me to get home in time for a late lunch of Cocoa Puffs and a peanut butter sandwich.

I heard the thunder first, rumbling its way through the world above. I didn't place the sound right away; it'd been some time since a good thunderstorm had passed through—so much so that it took me a moment to recognize it. Before long the tap-tap-tap of drops on the window announced the arrival of the glorious wetness. The heat that had been swelling up outside almost immediately gave way to a refreshing coolness, and I opened the curtains to let the welcome gusts of rain-soaked wind flush their way through my condominium.

By then we had a full-fledged storm roiling outside, so I quickly had to adjust my plan and leave the window open only a crack to avoid the regular sprays of moisture sluicing through the opening. But it was enough, and I sat nearby, enraptured by watching the water fall like someone had emptied a tumbler right above my building.

After a moment, the most severe torrents relented, leaving a pleasant, steady drizzle that swept across the sky and seemed to wash down the drains in the street the sweat and dirt and grime that had been accumulating over many days of heat and summer.

And, right before my eyes, children began to dance in the streets. Somewhere, some tired parent or babysitter had released her charges into the afternoon squall, and now they were laughing and jumping and splashing through puddles as if nothing else in the world mattered; as if rain were gold that had fallen from the sky and landed squarely in their very own toy box of a neighborhood.

I envied them.

At that moment, nothing else mattered to those kids. They were, of course, soaked in seconds. But they didn't care. They held races, splash contests, and tried to catch raindrops in wide-open mouths aimed up toward the heavens. Deep within me a yearning for that kind of long-lost joy welled up. But instead of joining them, I did the adult thing and watched, and smiled, from a distance.

The rainstorm didn't last long—twenty-five, maybe thirty minutes at most. But it left behind a world that was swept clean, and when the sun began to poke through the clouds above, that world sparkled with a freshness that inhabited all the senses. Below me on the street, the children didn't seem to notice that the storm was over. They kept on playing and dancing in the aftereffects of the rain. In an hour or two, they'd notice that their clothes had dried, that their toes were now squishing a bit uncomfortably in their shoes, and maybe they'd head inside for a snack or to watch TV. Maybe.

I turned away from the window and did what I should

have done from the first. I retrieved my trusty Nikon, aimed the lens through the curtains of my condo and captured on film the quiet joy of children at play. When I'd used up the roll, I developed the film in my darkroom. Not long after that, I was at Matthew's apartment a full ten minutes before our 6:00 appointment.

Jackson stood at the top of the stairs, apparently lost in his own thoughts about the earlier rain. He nodded my direction as I walked up the steps and turned toward number 23.

"Nice rain, huh?" I said in greeting. He favored me with a rare smile in response.

"Yeah. Very refreshing."

I motioned toward the apartment door. "They in there?"

"Yep. They're expecting you, so you can just walk right in."

"Thanks."

"Oh, and Todd?"

"Uh-huh?"

"She let Matthew pick out his own clothes again."

I chuckled. "Thanks for the warning."

"Figured it was my duty."

When I entered the apartment, Calia was singing in the kitchen. She had a nice voice; not timid, but not showy either. Firm and unafraid, with dead-on accuracy. But also soft, and unassuming, even in the higher register. I didn't recognize the melody, but stopped to eavesdrop for just a moment anyway. I should've known better, because as soon as I did she peeked around the corner and cut off her music mid-sentence.

"Pretty hard to sneak up on an angel, Todd."

I shrugged. "Can't blame me for trying, can you?

Is Matthew around?"

"He's in the bedroom. He'll be out soon enough. Thirsty?" She produced a tall glass of lemon-water. "Made fresh with rainwater caught just today," she enthused.

"Great!" I took the glass and moved toward the futon to wait. I noticed that Calia had set my drawing tablet and a few pencils there as well. I gave her a questioning look.

"In case you feel like drawing again," she smiled.

I set down my drink on the chrome edge of the coffee table and picked up the tablet. Inside it were the two sketches I'd done previously of Matthew.

"OK," I said. "Stand still for a minute, will you?"

I made a quick stroke on the paper, trying to imitate the wave of hair that flowed carelessly, but perfectly, down Calia's neck. She laughed, "Oh, not me, silly. Draw something else this time. Here."

She swung open the curtains, and from where I was sitting on the futon, I had a clear view of Jackson through the window. He stood motionless, almost like he'd been chiseled out of plastic or something.

Calia motioned toward her comrade in angelhood. "Draw Jackson," she said. "You may want to remember him someday."

"What do you mean?"

"That's for me to know, and you to find out." She giggled like a little girl and returned to the kitchen, humming softly.

I looked hard at Jackson for a few moments. He didn't stir, just stood leaning against the railing staring down the stairwell at who knows what. If I squinted I could just make out the belly of his shirt rising and falling with each breath he took, but other than that, he appeared to be a statue.

I flicked open a new page in the tablet and lightly sketched the outline of his head and hair. He moved then, and his face was out of view, but he stood up straight with his arms crossed. Still looking. Something about him looked almost majestic and fierce at that moment. Oh, he still had that "average white guy" physique and clothing. But it was almost as if he were wearing a disguise.

I started drawing in earnest, then. For some reason, I no longer saw him in the jeans and T-shirt combo he was wearing, but in a combination commando/Roman soldier outfit. So that's what I drew. As a finishing touch, I added a sword, held in his crossed arms, with the point down and resting on the ground.

"I wondered when you'd finally figure it out," a voice spoke in my ear.

"Matthew. I didn't hear you come in. How long have you been watching me?"

He reached to shake my hand, his grip strong and warm. I have to admit I did a double take when I saw him. For some reason, Calia had let Matthew dress in a 1920s style swimsuit for me. You know, the kind that makes it look like a guy is wearing long underwear with black and white stripes all over his body. It was not a pretty sight.

"About a half hour, I think. But it was fascinating to watch you work."

"Photography is work. This is just doodling."

"Well, it's very good 'doodling' then."

I looked out the window again, and Jackson was gone. "Well, guess my drawing session is over."

I started to say something else then, but that was when Matthew's first comment finally sunk in.

"What do you mean, you wondered when I'd 'figure it out'?"

He moved across the room and took a seat in the wing-back chair. "I wondered when you'd figure out who Jackson is."

I looked at my drawing again, then tried to piece together what I'd noticed about the other angel. Things started falling into place in my head.

"Well," I said slowly, "I'm guessing he's your body-guard."

Matthew and Calia both let loose with laughter then, and I immediately felt myself flush red. That made me feel even more stupid. I mean, this guy was wearing long underwear for goodness sake, and I was the one that was embarrassed?

"Close, friend Todd. But not quite. Some things can only be seen clearly through the eyes of a child. But you're close."

"What's that supposed to mean?"

The Apostle ignored my question, then, and out of apparent pity changed the subject.

"So, are you hungry? Should we head over to Del Taco for a chicken burrito or something?"

The mental image of me, walking next to a 1920s swimsuit, in public, made me shudder with fear.

"Um, no. Thanks. Had a late lunch, so I'm good."

"Did you enjoy the rain today?"

"Yes. Very much. In fact, I took some pictures."

I removed the freshly developed photos from their pouch and began laying out my pictures of children play-ing on the coffee table. Matthew responded with true delight, picking up each image for closer examination. Finally he said, "So, you did peek through the eyes of a child today, didn't you? No wonder."

"No wonder what?"

"No wonder you're ready to talk about faith."

I have to say, one of the more annoying things about my time with Matthew and Calia and Jackson was their ability to predict, or "read" my thoughts and intentions. This, of course, was one of them.

"I was just curious," I stammered, "about children playing in the rain. About how they could enter the storm without fear and soak up not just the wetness, but the joy of the moment as well. But that has nothing to do with faith."

Matthew reached into the pile of photos and pulled out a picture. It was of a little girl—maybe five years old—racing through a brand new puddle, arms outstretched, screeching in happiness as the water splashed up around her waist.

"No, Todd. It has everything to do with faith. Look at this girl. Why do you suppose she can revel in something as simple as rain, while you must experience it from a distance, through a camera lens?"

I sighed. He continued.

"Because as far as she's concerned, this entire thunderstorm was created just for her. It is God's special gift to a little girl. And she's right. It took a childlike faith for her to be able to recognize that truth."

He glanced up at me with a disapproving look. "You, on the other hand, are an adult. You've seen hundreds of rains. You know that a storm like this can also bring floods and wind damage and who knows what else. You can't see fully the gift that God has made for you in this rain. Your adulthood had put cataracts on your faith, blinding the childlike vision of truth that is there for all to see. But the little ones have made you curious. And that's why you want to talk about faith today."

I wanted to argue with him, to tell him he was all wet (so to speak). But the words he spoke rang true within me, and I decided not to fight it this time.

"Well, OK. You're right. I am curious about faith. I mean, let's be honest. I have a hard time having faith in God—not faith that he exists. That seems evident. But faith that he cares, that he is everything people say he is.

But here's the paradox, Matthew. I look at you, and I have to admit I believe you are who you say you are. I guess that takes a certain amount of faith, doesn't it?"

"Yes, Todd, it certainly does."

"All right, then. Let's talk about faith."

"What's your question for today?"

I took a moment to collect my thoughts.

"My question is this: What is true faith? And how does one get it?"

He leaned back in his chair, seeming to relish the moment before us.

"That's a topic that's hard to explain straight out. Faith encompasses many things. It includes trust and confidence and security and knowledge of the truth and so much more. Perhaps the best way to understand it is not to define it, but to look at it."

"What do you mean?"

"I remember once, when I was traveling with Jesus through the land of Judea. We stopped because so many people had come out to meet him, to beg healing of him, and to ask him questions like the ones you have asked me. May I tell you that story, Todd?"

"Knock yourself out."

He smiled this time, and leaned forward in the wing-back chair, assuming the role of storyteller as he had done when he related his own history to me weeks before. Once again, he began speaking in third person, relating his story as though it were someone else's.

"I will start with the crowd this time. With the mass of people pressing in, demanding a moment with the Christ ..."

There must have been thousands of them: men, women, young, old, sick, crippled, healthy, and religious leaders positioning themselves in places of prominence, as mindful of the crowd as they were of the Christ. Children raced through the mass of people, playing and enjoying the festive atmosphere.

There were thousands of them. And Matthew was tired of dealing with them. They'd come to the Master, to weep and beg for mercy. And he would heal them. Always. Then they'd run away to new life, forgetful of the one who had just freed them.

And those religious folk. What they wanted more than healing was status with the people. So they'd push their way to the front and, with mock respect for Jesus, ask some well-thought-out trick question intended to trip him up, make him look bad—and make the religious elite look better.

Still, he was unmoved. He answered their questions, one by one, explaining their need, reminding them who was God and who wasn't.

But it was getting late. And Matthew was tired. Surely the Master was tired too!

It was one mother and father first. "Look here," they said to Matthew and the other disciples. "Here is my son. Make your Christ bless him for me."

Another parent heard, and chimed in. "See, and tell him to bless my three daughters too!"

And another. "What of my children? I have four boys, strong and worthy. Tell Jesus to bless my boys too!"

It was too much. The boiling point had been reached. "Away with you all!" shouted Matthew. "Can't you see that Jesus is a very busy man? Bless your own children, and leave the Master alone. Go on now! Go!"

The hand on Matthew's shoulder silenced the apostle and the small crowd of parents and children around him.

"My Lord," Matthew mumbled. "I was just sending these children away, for surely you have more important things to do than—"

The Master shook his head ever so slightly then and spoke. "Let the children come to me, and do not hinder them, for the kingdom of heaven belongs to such as these."

And he welcomed them into his arms, each and every one. And they ran to him like a child runs to a parent after a long day away. The Master shunned the adults then, and the parents and disciples could only watch in amazement at the way those children hung on his every word. After he prayed for them, Jesus went away. But his promise to the children remained on their hearts and lips.

"Did you hear what Jesus said?" one boy called to his sister. "The kingdom of heaven belongs to you and me!"

The girl jumped up and down in excitement before grasping her brother's hand and leading him away. "We must go tell our friends. Let's go!"

Matthew watched them leave, and wondered. These older folk, the religious leaders and many others came to Jesus with distrust and envy and greedy hearts. They would not—could not—believe the promises this Christ made to them. But the children, oh, the children. A simple word, a gentle touch, and they knew that what Jesus promised them was truth, undeniable, undoubtable. Through the eyes of the child, matters of faith became clear, and the promise became a guarantee.

Matthew leaned back in the wingback chair and sighed. "So what is faith, Todd? I cannot explain it the way it should be explained. But I can tell you this: faith is what happens when a child believes a promise. And that kind of faith can only be defeated when a grownup can no longer see with the eyes of a child."

I sat quietly for a moment, trying to soak in what Matthew had just told me. I caught myself wishing—praying perhaps?—that I too could have the faith of a child.

Maybe someday, with practice, it would come.

I glanced down at my drawing of the faceless Jackson on my sketchpad.

"I see now," I said. "At least a little bit."

I took a long look at Matthew, then made a decision.

"Hey, let's head over to Del Taco after all. All this thinking has made me hungry."

He smiled.

It was the best chicken burrito I'd had in quite some time.

• • •

"That's far enough, young man!"

My mother has that nervous shrill in her voice, the kind of tenseness that indicates something has scared her just a bit.

"Aw, Mom! I just got started up this tree, an' look—I can reach that next branch easy!"

"Todd, no. You're already too high as it is. And there are dead branches all around you. One of them could break, and then you'd fall and hurt yourself."

I pause to glance at the ground below me. I am about fifteen feet up—an enormous distance to my five-year-old senses. Maybe she's right. I certainly don't want to fall.

"How 'bout just one more branch?"

"Todd." She frowns at me. "I said no. Now come down. Right now."

I look back at the ground, and suddenly feel dizzy. I cling more tightly to my branch.

"Come on, Todd. Come down now."

I start to reach my foot toward a lower branch, but it is a dead one and before I can put my full weight on it, I feel it break off and drop below me.

"Todd!" There is that shrillness in her voice again.

I am more than a little concerned now. I hadn't considered that climbing up would mean I'd also have to climb down. I twist a bit, trying to get a better look at the branches below me. A smaller twig is disturbed by my movement. It too falls to the ground.

"Todd," my mother says in what I think is a calmer voice. At least, it sounds like she's trying to be calm. "Don't move. Just stay right there. I'm going to get your father."

I feel an irresistible itch on my nose, but I am using both my hands to hold myself to the tree. So I gently rub my nose on the bark of the tree. In the process of satisfying my itch, I feel the sharpness of a scratch across the bridge of my nose. Tears spring out immediately as the sting of the cut registers in my brain.

"Todd, you're OK. Everything's going to be fine."

My father has arrived. He was across the park, talking to a family from our church. I feel myself relax at the sound of his voice. My tears dry up, and I smile.

"Hi, Daddy! Look how high I climbed!"

He smiles back at me. "I see. Very good job. Can you come down now?"

"I don't know. The branch I was using broke off."

"OK, Todd. Stay there for just a minute." I twist my head to follow his movement. In a few seconds he is directly below me, and I feel so tall to be looking down on him like this.

"OK, Toddles," he says. "Let go of your branch and fall. I'll catch you."

"What?" my mother has a wild-eyed look in her face. "Are you crazy? What if you dro—"

"I'm ready Todd. One, two, three—let go!"

I release my grip on the tree and fall laughing into my father's outstretched arms. His grip turns into a big bear hug before he sets me safely on the ground. "Now, no more climbing today, OK, Little Man?"

"OK, Daddy."

My mother is by my side now. "Are you OK? You scratched

your nose. You're so brave! You didn't even hesitate when your dad told you to let go."

"Daddy said he'd catch me," I say matter-of-factly before running to play on the swings.

Only later do I realize the leap of faith I had taken. Much later.

Perhaps too late.

• • •

We Talk about Greatness

THE MAIL CAME EARLY on the day of my next visit with Matthew. I was actually headed out to Whittier to meet the Apostle for lunch when I saw the postal worker's jeep drive away from the curb.

I don't know what it is about me, but I find it practically impossible to walk away from my occupied mailbox. Whenever somebody poses that age-old question, "If there were a fire in your home and you could only take one thing out with you, what would it be?" I usually make up some generic, admirable answer. But inside I know what I'd really take—the mail. I guess that's just a reflex from working so many years as a freelance photographer. If I'm doing my job correctly, then hopefully that mailbox will contain a paycheck with a fat photographer's fee or a new contract or a copy of some magazine spread I did or something like that.

Or maybe it's something else entirely. I had an old girlfriend in college who insisted I write her at least one letter every week—even though we saw each other practically every day anyway. Whenever I'd grumble about my ongoing assignment, she'd give me an ever-so-serious look and carefully intone, "Todd—a day without mail is like a day without sunshine. You wouldn't want me to go without sunshine would you?"

Corny, I know. But how could I say no? So I'd write the letters. Sometimes short, funny ones. Occasionally long, gushy ones. Mostly, just chatty, friendly ones. And, to her credit, she did the same for me. Sometimes we actually sit in the school library or a fast-food place together and write each other letters right then. When we finished, she'd always produce two stamps (she carried them in her purse; said it was a necessity since you never knew when you might have a mail-related emergency). She'd attach stamps to our now-sealed envelopes, and then we'd walk together to the nearest mail collection box and drop them off. Though I never admitted it to her, I always looked forward to receiving her letters in the mail. Oh, they were rarely anything of any depth or life-shattering importance. But they made me feel special anyway, so I saved them for the very last thing I'd open on the days they came, savoring the isolated moments that accompanied the reading of her words.

We dated less than six months before breaking up, but we remained great pen-pal friends for years afterward. I still smile when I get a rare Christmas card or birthday greeting from her.

And maybe that's the real reason why I can't sneak past my mailbox when I know it holds a hidden treasure (more likely, it'll be a few bills to pay).

So when I saw the mail carrier drive away I felt torn. Should I pause long enough to open the box and check what came this day? Or continue on my way to Matthew's, confident the hidden treasure in my box would wait patiently for me to return?

It was no contest. My feet overruled my brain, and in a moment I was fitting my key into the lock on the mailbox, swinging open the little door to find out what was behind it.

Bill. Bill. Junk mail. Magazine (was I in it? Yes! My shot

of a milk-mustached celebrity asking "Got milk?" looked very nice on page 17). A residual check for a photo reprint I'd authorized. And what was this?

The oversize envelope that caught my attention was from the Greater Los Angeles Greatest of the Year Committee. The printing on the outside proclaimed, "Time Sensitive: Ballot Enclosed." I stuffed all the other mail back into the box. (Now that I knew what was there, I could safely leave it for later pickup and not lose my sanity!) The ballot I stowed in a pocket of my shorts, figuring I might be able to sneak a glance at it while waiting at stoplights on my way up to Whittier.

The GLA Greatest of the Year awards are always fun for me. In fact, I even won a GLAGY award once in my illustrious career (1998—"Greatest Billboard Photo or Artwork"). Every year the committee sends out about 2,000 ballots to media professionals, critics, and anybody else lucky enough to land on the voter's list. Then we all vote for whatever we think was the "greatest" in a variety of categories: greatest advertisement, greatest news story, greatest reporter, greatest movie, greatest book, and so on. Then they have a big banquet in January of the following year to kick off awards season and tell everybody what we in the SoCal area think are the greatest things of the past year.

I already knew I hadn't been nominated for any GLAGYs this year, but was terribly curious to see if anyone I knew had been. Unfortunately, traffic, which is normally so bottled up and leisurely, refused to cooperate this day, and I barely had a chance to tear open the envelope before I arrived outside the Breezewood Arms.

Jackson stood at the curb, apparently waiting for me. He gave me a short wave and motioned toward an open spot on the street where I could park my car.

"Hello, Todd," he said as I got out. "Good to see you again."

I gave Jackson a quick look before replying. Something about this angel was both a little unsettling and yet comforting. Finally, I understood what Matthew and Calia had been talking about the previous week. But I wasn't sure if I could believe it or not after all.

"Hey, Jackson," I said. "The old man upstairs?"

He surprised me by shaking his head. "Not yet. But he will be soon. Do you want to wait down here, or go on up to the apartment?"

The sound of a car door slamming interrupted our conversation. "Hey, Jack!" a cheerful voice called out. "Out slumming again?"

I turned to see Miranda-the-next-door-neighbor walking up the sidewalk with two bags of groceries in her hands.

Jackson favored her with one of his rare smiles. "Hey, girl. Just getting my friend set up for the day," he said with a nod my direction.

"Aah, yes," she dimpled. "The guy with the loud knock. It's Todd, right?"

"Yes. Nice to see you again, Miranda."

She cocked her head back toward Jackson. "This guy tells me you're a photographer. So are you using that empty apartment for a studio or something?"

"Something like that."

"Cool. Listen, I'm looking to get a few photos taken of me and my kid brother for an anniversary present for my parents. Do you do any of that kind of thing? Or are you more the 'artsy' kind of photographer that takes pictures of rusty lug nuts and stuff?"

I laughed in spite of myself. "Well, I kind of do both."

"Great. Maybe we can arrange a time for a sitting or something? That is, if you're not too expensive."

"Sure," I said, feeling just a little embarrassed, like I'd agreed to a date or something. "And for a friend of Jack's, it's no charge."

She raised her eyebrows in happy surprise, and nudged Jackson with her shoulder. "Ooh, you are a good man to know, aren't you Jack? Now if only one of you big strong, empty-handed men would be kind enough to offer to help me with these groceries, my day would be complete."

"Of course. Sorry," I mumbled, feeling embarrassed even more as I reached for her bags.

"I'll get the last ones from the car," Jackson said.

"Thanks, Jack! And thank you, Todd. My arms were killing me."

We started up the stairs, then Miranda stopped abruptly. "Ooh, wait just a sec. The mail's here!" She bounced down the stairs to the mailbox area and quickly retrieved a handful of letters and junk mail. "Sorry," she smiled, "I'm an addict for mail. As far as I'm concerned, a day without mail is like a day with chocolate. And what's the use of a day like that?"

"My sentiments exactly," I said.

Jackson joined us then and we all walked our way up toward her apartment. "So, how long have you known this lug?" Miranda chatted up the steps.

"Who, Jackson?" I stole another quick look at the angel. "Well, I guess you could say he's been looking after me for about as long as I can remember. That sound right, Jack?"

Jackson returned my look, and something unspoken passed between us. "Yeah, Todd. I'd say that about covers it."

Miranda dimpled again, "Yeah, old Jack's a regular guardian angel, huh Todd? At least he has been for me. Well, here we are!" She unlocked the door to her apartment and turned to collect her grocery bags. "Thanks, you two! Want to come in for a soda or something?"

"Some other time, Miranda," Jackson said. "Todd's supposed to meet somebody next door in just a few minutes, so we'd better go."

"OK, then. Thanks again, guys. See you later Todd."

The door closed behind her. "Nice girl," I said to Jackson. He just nodded and appeared as if he were trying to hide a smile.

"You can go on inside number 23," he said in reply. "Matthew and Calia will be here shortly."

"What about you?" I asked.

"Oh, I'll be around."

As usual, I thought. And I found that thought to be comforting.

I had only been inside Matthew's apartment a few moments before Calia and the Apostle came laughing through the door. Today he looked almost normal. He wore a pair of baggy nylon gym shorts and a plain white T-shirt. Atop his head sat perched that Disney hat I'd given him, now starting to look more like an old friend, as a baseball cap should. Instead of his trademarked sandals, he was wearing a new pair of basketball shoes that looked comfortable and springy. In moments, Calia had tall glasses of water for each of us.

"Greetings, friend Todd!" Matthew reached out a hand toward me. I shook it, finding his grip to be strong as ever.

"Hello, Matthew. Nice duds."

He looked at me quizzically, so I motioned to his outfit.

"Oh, yes. Very comfortable. I could get used to this, you know."

"Been out for a bit?"

"Learned a new game today. A few boys from the

neighborhood invited me and Calia to play basketball at a court a few blocks over. Seemed like fun, so we went. They were better than us—"

Calia snorted.

"Let me rephrase that. They were better than me. Calia held her own quite nicely." He allowed himself a deferential nod toward the lady. "Better, my dear?" She nodded approvingly, and Matthew continued as we all took seats in the living room. "But I enjoyed the game."

"So you're not quite Michael Jordan yet, huh?"

"Who?"

I'd become so used to Matthew that sometimes I forgot he wasn't from around here—or even from around this "when."

"Michael Jordan," I repeated. "A lot of people consider him to be the greatest basketball player ever. He could do it all—dunk, shoot from the outside, rebound, pass, play defense. In his prime, he was the total package. Got more than a handful of championship rings to prove it too."

Matthew got a bemused look on his face. "What's that in your pocket?" he asked.

"Oh, this? A ballot. Since I'm a member of the media, I get to cast my votes on what are the greatest examples of—" I stopped, noticing that Matthew's bemused look was still there.

"What?"

"How do you define greatness?" he said.

"Well ..."

I looked down at my ballot, flipping it open for a closer look. The normal categories were there, along with a list of names. Some I recognized, some I didn't.

"What do you mean? Are you talking about in general, or politics or sports or what?"

"How do you define greatness?"

I frowned.

"Well, usually a greatest person is whoever is the most popular, or influential I guess. Or powerful. You know, like Michael Jordan or a king or a politician or a celebrity or something."

Matthew didn't respond, just sat there. Waiting.

"Actually," I said, "many people would consider you a great person. I mean, you are famous. Your writings have lasted millennia, and your thoughts are still a major influence in most parts of the world."

He chuckled softly at the thought, and shook his head gently. "That's all very interesting, Todd. But you still haven't answered my question. How do *you* define greatness?"

I dropped the ballot on the coffee table in front of us and frowned again. How did I define greatness? I'd known too many unethical politicians to think that holding political office made a person great. Influential, maybe. Great? No, not necessarily. Same for celebrities, and wealthy folk. A lot of powerful people in those categories; not that many great men and women though.

"I think," I said, "that we have our question for today. What is greatness?"

He nodded slowly. "It's a good question. An important question, I think. Because deep inside we all want to be 'great.' And until you and I know what that really means, we can never achieve greatness."

"You mean even one of Jesus' apostles wishes for greatness?" I said, teasing. He responded in all seriousness.

"Oh, yes. We all did, really. In fact, that was a big motivation for most of us who followed Christ back then."

"Really?"

"Yes indeed, Todd. You see, Jesus was a dynamic teacher. And he worked so many miracles! But if I am honest, many of us also secretly expected that he would be the future king of Israel. We envisioned him as a conquering leader, a man powerful enough to lead us into overthrowing the oppressive Roman government that kept us under its thumb. And when he became king, we all expected to be amply rewarded ourselves, with power and influence. Greatness, we thought."

"Wow. I never knew that."

He grinned. "Goodness, yes. We were just as greedy and self-absorbed back then as people are today.

"I remember once when James and John started making plans for their political futures. They held many whispered conversations about it. They tried to conceal it from us, but we all knew what they were talking about. We just didn't expect them to try to wrap things up so quickly.

"Back in my day, it was often not in good taste for a man to make a direct request for a favor himself. A friend, a supporter, someone respected who might speak on your behalf was a better tactic. And who more welcome than a mother? At least that's what James and John thought.

"So they enlisted the aid of their mother and sent her to ask Jesus a favor of greatness. 'Master,' she asked ever so humbly, 'Grant that one of these two sons of mine may sit at your right and the other at your left in your kingdom.'

"If I had known then what I know now, I would have pitied both the sons and the mother. At the time, though, all it did was make me angry. Mainly because I didn't think of asking for that first. But I didn't understand.

"He was gentle with her, but also firm in declining her request for great power to be granted to her sons. For Jesus, greatness had nothing to do with sitting on thrones or wielding much power."

The Apostle paused and took a sip on the glass of water before him. He fell silent for so long, lost in his thoughts—I grew concerned that he might have forgotten me and the end of his story. But now I was terribly curious.

"Matthew?" I said quietly. "What happened next?"

He returned his attention to me and shook his head with a bit of sadness. "We were so blind then. And he was so patient with us, teaching us like stubborn children who couldn't see what was right before our eyes."

"What do you mean?"

"Think about it, friend Todd. We were sitting in the very presence of the greatest person ever. The one whose own hands had created the universe and everything in it. The one who had formed the inner being of each one of us there, who had called us to himself. Yet Jesus never treated us as though we were merely his lowly subjects. Instead, the Lord of all gave up his heavenly majesty to wallow in the muck of humanity, reaching out with God's grace to every one of us.

"So, since we did not see what was plainly before us, he gathered us together and made it clear. 'You know that the rulers of the Gentiles lord it over them ... Not so with you. Instead, whoever wants to become great among you must be your servant, and whoever wants to be first must be your slave.'

"And suddenly it was so obvious. We found him to be great not because he could do miracles, but because the miracles he did were in service to helpless, hurting people who could never begin to repay him for relieving their pain. He was the greatest among us, and he was servant to us all—even to a wicked, greedy tax collector. And that, friend Todd, was true greatness."

I thought briefly back to my trophy shelf at home, where a certain GLAGY occupied a prominent place. Whom had I served in winning that award? An advertising agency, I guess. Maybe a few stockholders with shares in that company product that my billboard promoted. Did that make me great, as that award suggested?

No. Not really.

"Matthew," I said finally. "By that standard, you do

have a bit of his greatness yourself, you know."

"How do you mean?" he asked.

"Well, you're here, aren't you?"

He reached over and patted me on the shoulder. "It's an honor to serve you, Todd. And to serve him by serving you."

"Thanks, Matthew. Thanks for coming."

We talked a bit longer, and then there was an unexpected knock at the door. Four junior high boys stood outside. One held a dirty orange basketball and sheepishly invited us to come out and play. We stayed out until it was just too dark to see the rim of the goal anymore. And it felt great.

• • •

I am standing ankle-deep in refuse, fervently wishing I were somewhere else—or at least that swearing were permitted in the presence of my dad. Unfortunately, neither of those scenarios is going to happen anytime soon, so I stuff my face inside my T-shirt and do what I do best in situations like these.

"Da-ad," I whine, "Come on! I'm suffocating here. This place reeks!"

He starts to laugh, then thinks better of it and covers his mouth with his hand. "Whew! You're right, Todd. We'd better not waste any time."

Like hundreds of other unlucky teenagers, I have been dragged out to the city dump to help my father dispose of eight days worth of garbage. It's amazing how much trash can build up in one family's home over that time.

The city's garbage workers are on strike.

"Boy, I'll be glad when Larry and Detron go back to work," my father says as he grabs a load of garbage out of the bed of our truck. I grab a second load and shake my head in amazement. I think my dad is the only person in the city who knows

the names of his garbage collectors. But he does know them, and he often stops to chat with them while they're at our house on their route.

"Why are they on strike anyway?"

"Well—hoof—it's kind of a long story," Dad says, flinging another load out of the truck. "The sanitation workers are of the opinion that they're not appreciated. That the mayor has insulted them, in fact. Seems there was a clerical error and several of the workers received an official invitation to a city banquet. The governor of California will be there, along with a bunch of other bigwigs in politics. When the mayor found out, he revoked the invitations of the sanitation workers. Apparently this banquet was for 'important officials' only, and that no one needed a 'smelly garbage man' to stain the proceedings."

I try to stuff my face even farther into my shirt, beginning to feel pretty smelly myself. Thankfully, we're nearing the end.

"So the head of the sanitation department took offense at that. Said he'd show the mayor just how 'important' his workers were to this city. And now we have the soon-to-be-famous garbage strike. According to Detron, they'll stay out until the mayor issues a written apology and an invitation to the banquet to every single employee of the city's sanitation department."

I shake my head in disbelief. Dad throws the last load into the stinking piles, and we don't waste any time getting back in the truck.

"You see, Todd," Dad says as he fires up the engine. "A lot of people have a warped view of who and what's important in life. You know, we could live without a mayor for a week. But take away the low-level civil servants like Larry and Detron, and this city is a mess—literally! It's the people who work behind the scenes that often matter the most. Don't forget that, OK kid?"

I nod, testing the air to see if it's safe to release my face from the collar of my shirt. As far as I'm concerned at that moment, guys who do the dirty service jobs like collecting my garbage are *now the greatest heroes in the world. I'm also pretty sure I never want to be one.*

Two days later, the mayor finally caves in and issues his apology. Later I hear that the garbage workers all had a fine time at the banquet. And that mayor? Lost the next election to the former head of the sanitation department.

As I recall, he never held public office again.

• • •

We Talk about Honesty

The marquee above the theater said "Eight Minutes." It was a late-late show—a 10:35 P.M. showing to be exact. But Matthew had suggested it, and I figured it would be nice if I let him choose the time and location of our Tuesday meeting for once.

I stood in front of the theater doors, waiting. It was a small place—only two screens, it looked like—that apparently catered to the college crowd down in Irvine. The folks in theater 2 were getting an 11:00 P.M. showing of *From Here to Eternity*. The Apostle and I were getting some experimental flick that was making the rounds through art house locales in California.

The weather outside was perfect—warm night with a gentle breeze flowing in off the ocean, which made my shorts-T-shirt-sandals combo a perfect choice. It seemed almost a shame to go indoors for a movie, but apparently Calia had explained to Matthew the power of the cinema, and now he wanted to experience it for himself. After looking through the newspaper ads, he had bypassed all the big-budget films and picked out this little movie, filmed by a group of UCLA students on a digital camera, showing late into the night in an out-of-the-way theater house in Irvine. But I didn't mind, really. It felt good to be out on a night like this, and I have to admit I was a bit curious to see how Matthew would react to the big screen.

Jackson appeared first, tapping me on the shoulder from behind and nearly making me spill a box of Jujufruits I bought to pass the waiting time.

"Nice night," he said calmly by way of greeting.

"Yeah. I assume Matthew and Calia are somewhere around here?"

"Um-hm. Had a little trouble finding a parking space, but they'll be here shortly."

I checked my watch. It was 10:15 P.M., still plenty of time to get in for the show. "OK. I went ahead and bought our tickets," I said.

"Thanks."

Every head turned when Matthew turned the corner arm-in-arm with Calia. The two of them were chatting and smiling and looked very much like an older professor out on a date with one of his graduate students. I heard somebody nearby mutter, "Lucky stiff," to a friend who responded, "Yeah, someday I'm gonna be rich enough to afford a woman like that." A third voice chimed in, "Let's just hope you're not ninety before you achieve babe magnet solvency like that dude!"

For his part, Matthew looked almost normal. He wore blue jeans and a short sleeve, collared shirt along with his familiar, worn-out sandals. But Calia did look particularly impressive this night. She wore a long blue sundress that accented her figure and a smile that seemed to light up the sidewalk every time she looked at Matthew. I wondered briefly if it was OK to find an angel physically attractive, then decided that was probably a question for theologians to worry about. I was content just to admire her beauty for a moment longer before Matthew greeted me.

"Greetings, friend Todd!" Matthew called out to me a

few steps away. "So tonight we will 'take in a movie,' as Calia says. I'm looking forward to it."

I took my eyes off the angel and reached out to shake Matthew's hand.

"You know, Matthew," I said. "We've only known each other a short time, but already it feels like we've been friends forever."

"Yes it does, Todd. And I'm glad."

"I have our tickets already. Do you want some popcorn or anything before we get our seats?"

We stopped by the snack bar on the way into the theater and loaded up on popcorn and caffeine, with a little chocolate on the side. The lights were dimmed inside, and our eyes quickly adjusted. I was a little surprised to see that the theater was already two-thirds full. Not bad for an obscure indie film.

We found four open seats toward the front of the room, about six rows back and to the right. As if on cue, the lights went black almost immediately after we sat down. The murmuring conversations quieted to whispers, then disappeared as a cola advertisement began to flicker on the screen in front of us.

Here goes nothing, I thought to myself. *Hope this at least is better than Letterman.*

The film started shortly thereafter, rolling credits in a surprisingly static way, with nothing but an empty chair in the background. The camera zoomed in slowly on the chair, then as the end of the credits disappeared, zoomed back out to reveal a blond woman standing to the side, staring straight at us.

"Eight Minutes," the woman said. "It's the name of this movie you're watching, and also an eternity of life captured on film. Anything can happen in eight minutes—or not happen. The choice is yours, really.

"And that's what this film is about. Choices. And time.

And the life that passes so quickly by."

The camera zoomed back in on the chair. It was a basic padded metal thing, the kind you'd find at a professional seminar or lined up in a row at a doctor's office.

"Over the course of several weeks," the woman's voice intoned over the screen, "we invited people from all walks of life to join us for eight minutes. Here. In this room. In this chair.

"We had no agenda, no requests except for eight minutes. And we left the camera running the whole time. One hundred and thirty-three people gave us their time. When we were done, we selected a dozen, put them together and made this film. And so, without further ado, I give you: Eight Minutes."

The screen went black for a split second, then reappeared, revealing the chair, placed in the center of an otherwise empty room. I glanced over at Matthew. His full attention was on the screen, but he was absentmindedly eating popcorn one kernel at a time.

The door to the room opened, and a middle-aged man in a business suit walked through it. He wore a tie that barely passed his third button, and an ample pair of pants that did nothing to disguise a beer belly and thundering thighs. "In here?" he asked someone outside the door. "OK. That's it? OK, then. Well, I guess I'll see you in eight minutes." He gave a nervous wave through the doorway, then the opening closed leaving the man alone with the chair.

He took a look around, then walked straight up to the camera and peered into the lens. The result was that we in the audience got quite a deep look inside his nasal cavity. (Thankfully, he had apparently blown his nose before filming.)

"Is this thing on?" he said to no one. Then his face disappeared, apparently following his body behind the camera. The sounds of clothing shuffling around went on for a moment, then he reappeared in front of the camera.

I can't believe I paid money to see this, I thought to myself. I checked my watch and determined to do my best to endure, for Matthew's sake. I stole a glance at him just in time to see the Apostle spew a kernel of popcorn out of his mouth, joining the rest of the audience in laughter.

When I looked back at the screen, I saw that the man had pushed down the waistband on his pants to create a "baggy" look, pushed up the sleeves of his suitcoat, and then crossed his arms and adopted a ludicrous scowl on his face, apparently trying hard to imitate a gangsta rap star.

"Yo, booyyyzzz!" he said to the camera. Then he laughed nervously and looked around to see if anyone was watching. Confident he was alone, he reassumed his pose. "Yeah, west coast baaayybee," he said with idiotic nasality. "Don't make me pop you, dog! Yeah, booyyyzzz, that's whut ahm talkin' 'bout. Huh! You def, dog! True dat! Unh!"

Then, much to the delight of the people on my left, he started a flabby, bouncy rap dance punctuated by his own drumbeat. I think he may have been adding in rap lyrics from time to time, but it was hard to tell with the "pish-crish-boom-chaching-crish" stream coming out of his mouth along with the steady waves of laughter from the audience. Every so often he abruptly stopped his performance to check his watch.

At about seven minutes and thirty seconds, this overweight little soul finally took a breath. He was dripping with sweat by now, and his suit was a rumpled mess. Nonetheless, he straightened out his apparel, pulled up his pants and wiped his sticky brow with a sleeve. By the time the door opened, he looked almost normal again. Almost.

"All right, then," he said to the unknown person outside the door. "So that's it, huh? Well, OK." He leaned back toward the camera and winked. "Later, dog!" Then he was gone.

Matthew was transfixed by now. He put aside the popcorn and leaned forward in his seat to see who would come next.

The door opened again, and this time a heavily tattooed and pierced young woman came through it. She didn't acknowledge anyone outside the room, and generally ignored it when the door closed behind her. She walked to the center of the room and sat in the chair, focusing her gaze on the camera lens in front of her. She sat ramrod straight, staring with defiance and anger toward those of us in the audience. She didn't move again, except to blink and breathe, until her eight minutes were up.

It was actually suspenseful, if the truth be told. Like one of those scenes where you just know that any minute now a gloved hand is going to crash through the glass and grab the unsuspecting star by the throat. We kept staring at her staring at us, waiting for something to happen, expecting it at any second. Once, the girl on the screen took an unexpected deep breath and more than one person in our audience actually stifled a scream of surprise.

When the door finally opened again, the girl stood, glared at the camera and then extended a few fingers in a rude hand gesture. Several people in the audience laughed then, and a few cheered. I chewed on a bite of chocolate and wondered what had made that girl so angry—and why I had watched her do nothing with such intensity for the last eight minutes.

I caught Matthew looking at me then, grinning. But he said nothing, and we both turned back to the screen to see the next person featured in this little experimental film.

Over the next hour-plus, we watched a mini-parade of

life. An older woman came in and spent her eight minutes reciting classic poetry. A full-fledged clown—makeup and all—showed off his juggling ability. A twentysomething guy in a nightclub-stylish outfit practiced a standup comedy monologue. A teenager sang an operatic aria, with only a few mistakes. And one woman in her mid-thirties sat in the chair, looked into the camera and merely cried away the stresses of her life for her eight minutes. More than a few of us cried along with her, to be honest.

When it was over, the audience stood and applauded—characteristically—for eight solid minutes. I found out later that had become a custom among audiences who viewed the film regularly.

Finally, it was past midnight, and I was exhausted emotionally and physically. We all exited the theater and found an all-night diner nearby where we could relax, sip coffee, and talk about our experience.

"You know, it's actually Wednesday now," I said as I swirled a sugar packet into my cup.

Matthew laughed. "Yes, I guess it is, isn't it?"

"Guess that means this appointment has officially run over its allotted time."

Matthew stopped laughing and gave me a serious look. "Not yet, Todd. But soon."

"What do you mean?"

"You know I can't be here forever. I already died once. I'd rather not have to go through that again."

"So, how much time do we have?"

"Enough. Tomorrow is never promised. But we do have tonight, right now. So let's take advantage of it."

"OK," I said, my mind whirring.

Of course I knew that Matthew wouldn't stick around here forever. But it was at that moment I realized two things. First, sometime over the past few weeks I had finally decided to believe this balding little man in front of me was actually the apostle Matthew, come back from the far reaches of heaven just to answer my questions. Second, losing him was going to feel a lot like losing my father.

"So, Todd," the Apostle said. "did you like the movie?"

"Actually, yes. Though I'm a little embarrassed to say it."

"Embarrassed ... Why?"

"I don't know. I just spent close to two hours of my life watching other people waste eight minutes of theirs. And I liked it."

He smiled. "You liked it because it was true. Not because it was a waste of time."

"What do you mean?"

"For eight minutes, each one of those people was set free to be whoever he or she wanted to be. To be the person their hearts long to be. For those eight minutes we got to glimpse it acted out on camera, and it rang true within you as a result."

"I suppose you're right. I wonder why we can't glimpse the truth more often."

"Is that the question for tonight?"

"I think it must be."

Matthew sipped from his cup while he collected his thoughts. Then he spoke. "Often," he said, "the truth is laid out plainly for anyone to see. I think, though, that even more often we don't want to see the truth, in ourselves or in others."

"You're talking about me, aren't you?"

"I'm talking about everybody."

"Is it always like that?"

"Not always. I remember one time when people caught a glimpse of the truth, and it was glorious! But it was also short-lived. Within a week they forgot the truth they had seen with their own eyes and believed a lie instead.

"But for those few brief moments, the world stood at the brink of the truth and welcomed it for what it was."

"What happened?"

"Believe it or not, it started with a donkey. We were outside Jerusalem. We'd been traveling for many days to reach the city. As we neared our destination, Jesus sent two of us ahead. 'Find a donkey,' he said, and so we did. When we saw that he was going to ride the animal, we laid our cloaks on the donkey's back to create a makeshift saddle.

"It should have been a silly sight. This great Rabbi, prophet, teacher riding a lowly beast of burden. But it wasn't. It was regal and solemn and proud. We knew right then that what we'd suspected for so long was true. This really was the *Christ*, the Son of the living God!

"In those days, generals often paraded into their home cities after winning a war. They would mount their battle horses and ride through the city, greeted by crowds and cheers and people waving palm branches in celebration of the conquering hero.

"Jesus was never a general, and his little donkey was certainly no warlike charger. But when it spread ahead of us that Jesus was coming to Jerusalem, he was greeted with a king's welcome.

"They came from everywhere, from every corner of the city. They crowded the streets and passageways. They shouted from rooftops and rained praises from the trees. They waved palm branches and sang songs. Their eyes were opened, and for this short time they could see what had been hidden from them for so long.

"God had come. The Lord had seated himself on a lowly animal, humbled himself and was now here to conquer the power of sin once and for all.

"It was a moment of truth, and we all saw it, recognized it, reveled in it. If only it would have lasted."

Matthew closed his eyes then, picturing the scene in

his mind's eye once again. He seemed to be swept away by the vision behind his eyelids, and quietly hummed a processional tune, "Hosanna to the Son of David! Blessed is he who comes in the name of the Lord! Hosanna in the highest!"

After a moment, he ended his praise song and looked at me again. "Truth is no secret, really. It is only hidden from eyes that refuse to look for it."

"You're talking about me again, aren't you?"

He sighed. "I'm talking about everybody, Todd. And yes, that includes you."

"I want to see the truth."

"I believe you do, Todd. And I believe you will find it."

"Before it's too late?"

Matthew didn't respond. After a moment Calia called for the waitress and paid our tab.

"It's late," I said. "I guess we should call it a night. I'll see you next week?"

For the first time, he looked tired to me. Were those circles under his eyes? I couldn't tell for sure.

"Wouldn't miss it for the world, Todd."

Jackson hung back after Matthew and Calia drove away. "Gonna be all right going home by yourself?" he asked. "Want me to ride with you?"

"No thanks, Jackson. I'll be fine. But thanks."

He nodded and started to walk away.

"Hey Jackson," I said. "Can I ask you a question."

"Sure."

"I'm curious. What does Matthew do when I'm not around? On Wednesdays or Saturdays or whatever?"

The angel looked at me for a moment, then shrugged. "Mostly," he said, "he prays for you."

• • •

"All right, Todd. Who did it?"

I sit at my desk on the front row of my Applied Sciences 201 class, ready to tackle the challenge that Professor Hightower has placed before me.

"Take your time," he says. "Look for anything you can use to help you see the truth."

He motions to the three students standing beside him at the podium. "I will tell you this," he says, "one of these friends of yours is a thief. Everybody here saw that person take your precious Mountain Dew can and guzzle it down while you were out of the room. Right class?"

My fellow students hoot their approval, obviously enjoying the little object lesson playing out before them.

"So the question for you, Todd, is which one did it? Which one is the true thief, and which are innocent bystanders carelessly slandered by those of us who know better?"

I stand and martial all my powers of observation to solve the mystery. My empty can sits, half-crushed, on the podium. I step up to Rick. He laughs nervously. "Dude, it wasn't me. You know I'd never stoop so low as to steal a guy's caffeine—especially not during an eight-o'clock class!"

His eyes flick restlessly from me to the can to the classroom filled with students watching him squirm in the harsh spotlight of suspicion.

I move to Ellen. "Not me, sweetie," she says sincerely, and then she raises her eyebrows and indicates with her eyes that I should finger Rick for the crime.

"Don't listen to her, Todd," RiAnn says, third in the lineup. "Ellen's the real thief. And man, does Mountain Dew make her burp or what?"

We all laugh, and Ellen looks appropriately indignant at the accusation. Could this petite, stylish girl be a thief in disguise? Naah. Not Ellen. And RiAnn's lipstick appears dry and untouched. Couldn't be her, either.

"All right," I say after a minute. "I'm ready."

"Are you sure, Todd?" asks the professor. "Want to run a test or anything? Have your suspects take breathalyzer exams or something like that? This is a science class, after all."

I shake my head. "No, I know who the criminal is," I say with certainty. "Rick, you owe me 75 cents for a new soda!"

"Du-ude!" Rick laughingly protests while the class cheers. "I didn't do it! I was framed! It was a setup!"

I hold out my hand for the coins. To my surprise, Ellen is the one who drops the three quarters into my palm.

"Sorry, Todd," she says sweetly. "But it sure tasted good anyway."

Everyone applauds as Professor Hightower sends us back to our seats. "So," he says, beginning his lecture. "As Todd and Ellen have so eloquently showed us, the truth is not always such an easy thing to see—especially when it relates to people we know. Here in our class today, that's a relatively harmless situation because good ol' Todd still gets some change to replace his stolen soda. But what about in a court of law? What about then? Mistaken realities there could send an innocent man to jail, or cost a woman her life! We have to have a way of discovering the truth in those situations, and that's where applied science comes in. Specifically, the sciences of fingerprint and DNA technologies ..."

I dutifully begin to take notes, but I am distracted by the fact that I was so easily fooled by Ellen. I've heard it said that the truth is out there. Now I'm wondering if I'll be able to recognize it when it really matters.

• • •

We Talk about Failure

I awoke the following Tuesday with a melancholy feeling that seemed to seep through my skin and into my bones. I'd slept long and hard, yet still felt tired, like I'd been running a marathon in my dreams.

To be honest, the feeling of melancholy had been establishing its hold on me for several days already, beginning the previous Sunday morning. I guess my Tuesdays with Matthew were finally starting to get to me, and maybe I wanted it that way. So, Sunday morning, for the first time since I don't know when, I got up early, put on a tie, and went to church.

I picked a large congregation in Fullerton, figuring I could easily slip in unnoticed, take in the service, and sneak out the back again without too much trouble. My plan worked like a charm. The place was packed with middle class America, all dressed in Sunday best, smiling, talking, singing. With rare exceptions, children had apparently been banished from the sanctuary and shuttled off to kids' church and young people's Sunday school classes. I have to admit that after the past few weeks with Matthew, I kind of missed the sights and sounds of childhood in this church. Made the place seem so adult, and only added to my feeling that I was out of place.

When the singing started, however, I felt right at home

again. Seems praise and worship music hadn't changed too much in the time since I'd been gone. Oh sure, there were some tunes I didn't recognize, and this church featured a full band instead of just my mom playing piano. But there were also enough melodies that I remembered from my dad's old churches that I even found myself singing along.

It was sometime during that singing that I felt the aching inside—a sadness that was both familiar and foreign, like the hollow stomach you get when you realize you've got no place to go for Christmas. No, not sadness really. Longing. An unfulfilled desire for … for something.

So I sang, even closing my eyes from time to time, searching within me to find that something that seemed to be haunting my emotions. But it was always just beyond my reach, just outside my vision, appearing and then whispering away when the music ended.

I barely heard the sermon after that, lost in my thoughts and the melancholy that threatened to overtake me. Memories I'd thought were not there began resurfacing in my mind, adding to the incompleteness I was experiencing. I thought of my father, of my many failings, and the way my life had turned out just liked I'd planned it—but without the satisfaction I'd expected to be there.

It reminded me of the Shakespearean play, Macbeth. My high school English teacher forced my entire class to read that play. I pretended to hate the task, just like everyone else. But each night I drank up the assigned reading, stumbling happily over the words to find out what would happen next in the story.

Now, this Sunday morning, I began to feel something like the Lady Macbeth. Guilty of conspiring in the murder of her king, she imagined her hands covered with his blood. She washed and washed and washed her hands, and yet still the stain of the deed lingered. "Out damned

156   Tuesdays with Matthew

spot! Out I say!" she cried in her madness. But always the blood remained. She was guilty, and "all the perfumes of Arabia" would never wash away the blood she saw in her own hands.

In my mind, as the preacher delivered his sermon, it was Lady Macbeth that spoke to me. She stood as my example and my accuser, for I too have my "damned spots" that no one can see. And no matter how hard I try to wash away my failings, to cover up my selfish wrong-doings, I still feel them, sense them crowding in. They crowd in on me that day from the brink of consciousness, reminding me what a feeble, sinful, sad little man I have become.

When church finally dismissed, I was the first into the aisle, heading for the door, wondering why I liked and hated this church service, both at the same time. Then I saw her. Miranda stood at the back, chatting animatedly with a few other ladies. She looked radiant, her ringlets tamed and pulled back behind her ears, her eyes flashing with excitement as she told whatever story it was she was telling. A sky-blue sheath dress accented her figure without going too far, and she wore those same heels she'd been hurriedly slipping into on the day we first met.

I shouldn't have been surprised to see her there. After all, this was a well-known church, and people drove in from all over to attend Sunday services there. But there I was anyway, feeling like a pimply teenager with a crush on the most popular girl at school.

I turned to find a different exit and discovered I was now the bottleneck between several hundred people who crowded the aisle and were trying to leave. So I mustered my courage and marched (nonchalantly, I hoped) up the aisle toward the door. Miranda caught sight of me almost immediately, and I have to admit I was glad to see that a smile accompanied her recognition. She bid goodbye to her friends, then waited for me to reach the back of the auditorium.

"Well, if it isn't Todd the photographer," she greeted warmly. "Nice to see you again."

I nodded and tried to return her smile. "Nice to see you again too, Miranda." Then I couldn't resist adding, "So, come here often?"

She laughed appropriately. "Yeah, been coming here for about four years, ever since I became a Christian."

I could see the question in her eyes, the curiosity about my own state of spirituality. But good manners prevailed, and she refrained from putting me on the spot just then. "Hey," she said instead, "a few friends of mine and I are headed over to CoCos restaurant to grab a bite to eat. Care to join us?"

I must have hesitated a little too long, for I saw her flush just a bit before she hurriedly added, "I mean if you haven't already got someplace else to go. And, you know, there'd be four or five of us there."

I nodded. "Yeah," I said, "no, I mean, it sounds like fun. But, well, I already made plans for this afternoon."

I don't know why I said that to her. I mean, I was obviously single, and she certainly seemed to be pleasant company. But deep inside I think I knew I wasn't going to be such good company myself this day, and spared her from having to discover that on her own.

"OK, sure," she said clumsily. "Some other time maybe."

"Yeah," I said. "Some other time." I excused myself. "Well, great to see you again, Miranda. Maybe I'll see you on Tuesday."

She smiled her goodbye, and I headed toward the monstrous parking lot outside. Turning down an almost-date with a pretty girl didn't help my attitude, and the sadness within me soured to bitterness that had stayed with me until the alarm went off on Tuesday morning.

One of the drawbacks of being self-employed is that there's no boss waiting around, telling you to get to work. No annual performance review that tracks your attendance and marks you down for days out. So when I rolled over and slapped the alarm that morning, I bypassed the snooze button and hit the "off" switch instead. I just didn't feel like getting out of bed that day, and nobody was around to make me. I rolled over and went back to sleep.

Around 11:30 A.M., nature finally prevailed and I rose long enough to take care of business. Then I put a CD in the player and went back to bed and back to sleep.

Around 3:15 P.M. I felt a cool touch on my cheek. I did not need to open my eyes to know who it was.

"Just once," I mumbled through clenched eyelids, "I wish you guys would knock."

Calia's tinkling laughter filled the room briefly, then was replaced by concern in her voice. "You OK, Todd? You didn't show up for your appointment with Matthew, so Jackson and I figured we should check up on you."

"I'm sick," I lied, faking a cough afterward. I peeked out at my angels. Jackson had a disgusted look on his face. Calia merely looked tolerant. "Tell Matthew I'll see him next week." *Maybe*, I thought as I finally opened my eyes all the way.

Calia took a step back and regarded me coolly. "All right, Todd. No one is going to force you to meet with Matthew. But I won't lie to him."

I pulled the covers over my head. "Fine," I said. "Just tell him I'm not coming."

When I dared to steal a look out from under my sheet again a few minutes later, the room was empty. I crammed shut my eyes and willed myself back to sleep.

How much time do we have?

Matthew shrugged. "That's not my decision to make. But I am here today, so let's take advantage of that, shall we?"

When I woke again at 4:30 P.M., I couldn't tell if I'd been dreaming or not. But Matthew's words nagged at my brain. How much time did I have left with the old man? What if today was to be the last day of this miraculous dispensation?

I felt nauseous, and my stomach growled. But it was the hunger in my heart that finally got me out of bed and into the shower. I was on the road by 4:45 P.M.—just in time for that famous Southern California rush hour traffic. I could only hope he wouldn't be gone by the time I got there.

The street was deserted when I finally pulled up to the curb outside the Breezewood Arms. I made my way up the stairs and stood for a moment outside apartment number 23. I could hear a faint television set playing from inside Miranda's place, but everything was dark and quiet before me.

He's already gone! The thought flashed through my head. *And I'm too late. Again. Story of my life.*

I stood in front of the apartment, not sure what to do. The sound of Jackson's voice startled me out of my indecision (and very nearly made me wet my pants).

"Here, I'll do it," he said from right behind my left ear. "Just so you'll know that I know how." He reached across my shoulder and rapped on the door, three solid—but respectably soft—knocks. Then he reached down and turned the knob, motioning for me to enter.

Matthew and Calia were inside, sitting in a dusky darkness. The setting sun outside illuminated enough of the room through the curtains, but the shadows were beginning to creep in around the corners.

Tuesdays with Matthew

I walked in and took a place in the director's chair. No one said anything for quite some time. I don't know how long, just that it was silent and that silence brought with it a measure of peace. I closed my eyes for a time. When I opened them, I found Matthew's eyes fixed on mine.

"Greetings, friend Todd."

"Hello, Matthew. Sorry I'm late."

He nodded deferentially. "Want to talk about it?"

"No."

He nodded again, and we let the silence rule a moment longer.

"I have a memory," I said finally, "that I'd really rather forget."

"We all do, Todd."

"He dropped me off at college, you know. Drove me to the dorm, helped me unpack my things. Gave me a hundred dollar bill too. Said it was for all the things we must have forgotten that I'd need to buy in the next few days."

"Did he give you the money before or after the argument?"

"After."

I shook my head. Sometimes it was really annoying to be around people who knew the deepest, darkest secrets of your life.

"What happened?"

"It was time for the goodbye. He gave me a hug and said, 'I'm proud of you son. I think you're going to really enjoy college. Your mother and I will miss you, of course. But I think this will be a great experience for you, and once you get hooked up with a good church, you'll—'

"'Dad,' I said. 'I think you should know, I won't be going to church anymore.'

"He didn't say anything at first, just looked at the floor in disappointment. Finally he said, 'I was afraid of that.'

"And that's when I let him have it. Years and years of bitterness just spilled out of me like water out of a faucet. I called him a fool, a pastor of hypocrites, and an intellectual idiot for wasting his life serving people who always ended up stabbing him in the back or complaining about his family or paying him too little to even afford a vacation away with his wife.

"I expected him to defend himself, to tell me to sew up my mouth or he'd sew it up for me. But he just listened.

"So I told him what I thought of his God and his religion and that I for one wouldn't condemn myself to the same fate.

"'Todd, you don't understand,' he said. 'Yes, sometimes we've had our share of troubles. And sometimes even Christians can act dishonestly and hurtfully. But it's not about them; it's not even about you or me. It's about Jesus, who he really is, and what he wants for you.'

"I reached out and shook his hand then, cutting him off before he could get into a sermon. 'Goodbye, Dad,' I said. 'I'll call you and Mom once a month, and will see you again at Christmas, I guess.'

"'Todd—'

"'*Goodbye,* Dad.'

"That was when he gave me the hundred dollars. He knew I'd just rejected him and his faith all in one fell swoop. And he still gave me the money. I spent it—and the money he sent regularly throughout my college years—without a second thought. Only now do I see he did that in spite of me, not because of me."

Matthew reached out and gripped my shoulder.

"We never talked about that conversation again, Matthew. Never brought it up, even when he was dying. But I know that from that point on, he always felt like something of a failure. And I did too."

"We all have failed, Todd. We all have fallen short."

"Yes, I guess so. But I seem to be particularly good at it. I don't have dozens of memories like that one, Matthew. I have hundreds. Maybe thousands. I have managed to hurt just about everyone who has loved me; even myself. And I think, even God. What hope can there be for a selfish, sinful man like me, Matthew?"

He nodded, and the silence took over the room again, just for a moment. The shadows cast by the setting sun were now getting longer, creeping away from the corners and toward the center of the room. But none of us made an attempt to turn on a light. Our eyes had adjusted to the growing dimness, and that was enough for the moment. Then Matthew spoke.

"I remember," he said, "exactly where I was the night before they killed the Christ."

"What?"

"It was a beautiful evening. Picturesque, almost. We had gathered in a room to observe the Jewish Passover holiday, a day commemorated with a ceremonial feast. Jesus himself was the master of the meal, and though he knew what was to come, he still served us, one by one, the bread and the wine.

"We sang a hymn of thanks taken from the book of Psalms, then set out walking to a nearby place, to the Mount of Olives. It was not a long walk, maybe fifteen minutes or so. The sky was clear and stars blazed like roaring fires in the heavenly distance.

"Then he stopped, turned and faced us all. I stood next to my friend, a fisherman named Peter. Jesus called him a 'rock,' and he was the obvious leader among those of us who followed Christ.

"Jesus looked straight at him, and at me. 'This very night,' he said, 'you will all fall away on account of me.'

"We stood openmouthed in shock. How could this be? We, all of us, had given up everything to follow the

Master, the Christ. We had been there when the crowds shouted his name, when they tried to make him king of Israel by force. Would we now run away? Absurd.

"Peter took Jesus' words especially hard. 'Even if all fall away on account of you,' he said. 'I *never* will.' And he meant it too. He vowed that he would rather die by Jesus' side than deny him."

Matthew gave a rueful smile that seemed especially appropriate in the gathering darkness of the room. "I made that same vow, Todd. We all did. I said I would die before disowning my Lord."

"You didn't, I take it?"

"No, Todd. When they came for him, I ran like a scared chicken. I ran and hid, buried myself in my home. I was scared they might come for me too if they knew I was one of his disciples. So I let him die alone. That was my failure, Todd. My greatest failure."

I heard the tears splatter onto the coffee table before I saw them, and only then did I realize how vividly Matthew could relive those moments.

"It happened millennia ago," I said weakly.

"Yes," he said. "And it happened just yesterday." He took a moment to compose himself before continuing. "My friend, Peter? At least he tried. He followed the soldiers and the judges to the place where Jesus was to be condemned. During the cold of the night, he tried to warm himself by a fire the servants had made. Then a little woman with a little knowledge was all it took to bring out his weakness.

"'You also were with Jesus,' she said. He did not hesitate. 'I don't know what you're talking about,' he said. As soon as the words left his mouth his heart began to mourn. A second servant challenged him. Again, he denied the Christ. But even his words gave him away, for he carried the accent of his birthplace. A Galilean drawl is hard to disguise, you know! And a third called him a friend of Jesus. Peter's fear consumed him then, and he cursed and shouted and denied that he ever knew 'the man.'

"A rooster crowed then, and Peter remembered Jesus' words to him only a few hours prior—and the empty promises he had made to his Messiah."

Matthew sighed. "It was a dark night for us all."

"And yet you made it through."

"Yes, Todd. I did. And so did Peter. And so will you."

"How can you be so sure?"

He didn't answer right away. Instead, he nodded to Calia who flicked a match from somewhere and lit a candle on the table in front of us. The flame flickered and leapt into life, bringing a kind of yellow-orange glow to Matthew's face nearby and chasing away the shadows that had crept over us after the sun had gone down.

"'What hope can there be for me?' you asked tonight, Todd. Your hope is the same one that carried Peter and me through that awful night when we let the worst in us show. Your failures, like mine, like everyone's, are many. But they are never too much for the forgiveness that Jesus offers to all who will ask for it."

"That seems so simple. Too easy."

"Maybe it is simple. But it was by no means easy. This is something I know from experience."

"The only real failure, Todd, is to miss out on the grace of God."

I felt something tugging at my melancholy then. Hope, perhaps? I watched the candle burn, wondering. Finally, Matthew stood and extended his hand.

"Time to go, I guess."

"It has been a long night."

"Will I see you next week?"

Matthew glanced over at Calia, and something unspoken passed between them. "Yes, Todd. But my time here is coming to an end. I think you should know that."

"How much longer do we have?"

The Apostle shrugged. "I don't know. But I do know we will have next week. So let's meet again, on Tuesday."

"I'll be here," I said, mustering a weak smile. "And I'll be on time."

Matthew smiled. "Think about what I said, Todd."

"I will, Matthew."

It was nearly midnight by the time I got home. I don't know if it was because I had slept away most of the day, or because my mind had a lot to work through, but I stayed up late into the night. Thinking.

• • •

I can feel the heat on my cheeks, burning me from the inside. I take a second look at the paper in front of me. Yes, that's my name at the top. And that means that the large, red "F" below it is mine too.

I steal a glance at Kylie Usher on my left. She is disappointed, but she still has earned a "B" on the exam. Ryan Holder to my right has made an "A."

My grade remains unchanged. It is still an "F." There is a note at the bottom of the paper, written in red ink, from the teacher to me.

"Todd," it says, "I want you to know that I saw you copying answers off of Kylie Usher's paper. That is the reason for your grade. If you'd like to talk about this, please see me after class."

I quickly flip the paper over on my desk to hide my failure from my classmates.

"Some of you may be disappointed by your performance on this first test," my ninth grade Spanish teacher is saying. She gives me a meaningful look. "Just consider it a reminder that

high school is going to require much more from you than junior high."

She continues passing the papers around the classroom.

An "F." For cheating. My heart sinks. My stomach feels slightly nauseous. How will I explain this to my parents?

Carefully I fold my test paper in half, and then in half again. One more fold and it fits inside my pocket.

I will hide my failure, I think. When I get home, I will tear this paper into little shreds and throw it in the trash. No one will ever know.

But I know. I always know. It is my secret, and it never goes away.

No matter what successes may come in my future, I am forever a ninth-grade cheater. A failure. Always.

• • •

We Talk about Love

THE STANDING WEATHER JOKE in my neighborhood is this: "Here in southern California we only have two seasons. 'Hot.' And 'Hotter.'"

I thought that was pretty funny until I heard it repeated by a local in Phoenix ... and in Dallas, and in Orlando, and in pretty much every other warm-weather state in the union. Then my respect for weather-related humor became all but nonexistent. Trouble is, the joke is true. We don't seem to have a real changing of the seasons here in SoCal, just more days that slip by on the calendar. So when the first Tuesday of September rolled around, I almost had to remind myself that fall had begun.

Folks in Colorado were already seeing the first tinges of orange and yellow on the trees. Back in Michigan, if the news reports were correct, they'd already traded in their summer shorts for jeans and windbreakers. But here in Newport Beach the sun just kept shining, the cool wind kept blowing in off the ocean, and we all took for granted that fall would be indifferent to us yet again, spreading itself to the rest of the nation and leaving us in our cocoon-like existence where summer and spring were all that we had.

My mood had improved since the last meeting with Matthew, and I was actually looking forward to seeing the

Apostle yet again today. The thing that kept nagging at me was the feeling that time was running out, that my little miracle would end too soon. I found it funny how quickly I had been sucked unto this situation that would seem delusional to just about anyone else who gave it a cold, hard look. But it didn't matter. I believed this man was truly the apostle Matthew, come back from the gates of heaven just to spend time with *me,* to answer *my* questions—and to spark new ones in my mind. Could I explain how that had occurred? No, not really. It was an impossible thing. But that also made it a miracle, and that something I wasn't willing to let go of … yet.

Just before I left Matthew's apartment the week before, Calia had handed me the sketchpad I'd used in weeks gone by. "You might want to keep this," she'd said to me.

"Why?" I asked. "I'm happy just to keep it here while I'm meeting with Matthew."

She just shrugged. "I think you'll want to keep it at your place from now on," she said.

So I brought it home with me and worried that it meant my time with Matthew was almost over. I flipped through the sketchpad after breakfast. Three pictures were in there, two of Matthew, one of Jackson. It seemed incomplete, so I took out a few pencils and opened to the next blank page.

I started out with the intention to draw Calia, at least what I could remember of her in the Hispanic angel guise she'd used throughout our time together. Midway into the drawing, I realized the face I'd drawn looked more like someone else, not quite the angel's features that I had envisioned in my mind. I kept working and, after a moment, realized that if I added ringlets to the hair the picture I'd drawn would bear a remarkable resemblance to Matthew's next-door neighbor. So I added the ringlets, and determined to take the notebook with me that afternoon when I met with the Apostle, to try to capture the angel on paper then. Better yet, I decided to also pack my trusty Nikon. Maybe I could sneak in a photo opportunity with the whole heavenly crew.

I had a little time to kill before leaving to meet with Matthew, and I'll admit I was bored. I'd scheduled myself off for this whole day, and for every Tuesday in the coming month, just in case. But I am an impatient soul at times and couldn't bear to simply sit and watch television until it was time to go. Having my camera packed and ready only added to my restlessness, so I did the first thing that popped into my mind.

There is a Pep Boys garage not far from my condo, so I called over there with an unusual request.

"Thank you for calling Pep Boys. How may I help you?" The attendant on the other end of the phone was polite, but also obviously busy.

"Hi, I'm just calling to see if you happen to have any, um, lug nuts for a car?"

"Yes, we do carry lug nuts," the attendant replied, and I could hear him tapping keys on a computer keyboard, apparently getting ready to look up part sizes for me. "Are you looking for regular lug nuts, or the theft-proof ones with their own special wrench?"

I hesitated. This was going to sound stupid. "Actually," I said, "it doesn't really matter what kind they are. Except they need to be rusty."

He sighed. "Is this a prank call?" he said, "because you sound a little old for that kind of thing, and I've got customers waiting at the counter here."

"No, no! I'm serious. I'm, well, I'm a photographer and I've got a client who is interested in a photo of, um, rusty lug nuts."

There was silence on the other end of the phone.

"You know these L.A. types," I said with blue-collar

sympathy. "Anything is art to them. And hey, if she's willing to pay for it ..." I drifted off, hoping I'd affected the right mix of seriousness and lightheartedness.

"Just a moment," he said finally, "I'll transfer you to the garage."

The mechanic I spoke with was actually an amateur sculptor himself and seemed interested in the concept. And believe it or not, they actually did have a set of five rusty lug nuts, pulled off a vehicle the day before and replaced with new ones. They let me have them for free (I guess there's not a huge market for rusty lug nuts over at Pep Boys), and I took them over to Newport Beach for a photo session.

Sure, it was goofy, but it did keep me busy until just after lunchtime, and that's all I really wanted at that point. I took several portraits and used up four rolls of film. There was "Lug Nuts on Holiday" which featured the rusty family nestled comfortably on a beach towel, shaded by bright red cocktail umbrellas. "Lug Nuts Sand Castle Derby" had the rusty ones posed proudly aside an award-winning, paper cup-shaped castle in the sand. "Surf Nuts" found the lugs tumbling off a boogie board after crashing onto the beach from a particularly gnarly wave. You get the idea.

When I was finished, I went to a nearby one-hour photo shop, tipped the guy an extra $5 to move my film to the front of the pack, and had my masterpieces in twenty-two minutes flat. I took the best shots and slipped them in a manila envelope with a note. What the note said was personal, and I won't share it here. But suffice it to say I was going to leave it outside Miranda's door and hope for the best.

Around 1:30 P.M., it was finally time to head up to Whittier. I grabbed a chicken whopper at Burger King on the way up, and made it to the Breezewood Arms at 2:40 P.M. Twenty minutes early, but I preferred it that way.

There was an envelope waiting for me outside the door to Matthew's apartment. I felt my heart seize. Was this the goodbye I'd been hoping to put off? I tried the doorknob to number 23 and found it locked for the first time since I'd been coming there. I dropped my rusty lug nut pictures in front of Miranda's place, then carried my own envelope downstairs back to my car.

Once in the driver's seat, I ripped open the manila clasp and found a note, apparently written by Calia:

"Todd," it said, "Matthew thought it would be fun if we met at The Fullerton Arboretum today. We already left to head over there, so come on out as soon as you get this note. We'll be looking for you! C."

There was a simple, hand-drawn map at the bottom of the page showing where the arboretum was in relation to the 57 freeway, but I knew how to get there anyway. It was a great place to photograph nature in bloom, and I had to admit I'd been there more than once.

When I spotted the Victorian cottage on the arboretum grounds about a half hour later, I knew I'd arrived at the appropriate place. I found Matthew and Calia admiring some unknown plant from the Sonoran desert out in that section of the acreage.

I felt lucky to find them so quickly, because at 26 acres, the Fullerton Arboretum could be an easy place to get lost. But the Apostle was hard to miss, decked out in bright orange shorts, a yellow sport shirt, and black suspenders. I couldn't decide if the mishmash of colors made him look really cool or just like a guy with no fashion sense. But I didn't care; I was just glad to see him again.

I didn't see Jackson, but had a feeling he was nearby anyway. I sneaked up behind Calia and Matthew and tried to listen in on their conversation, but it was all in

Aramaic, and I had no idea what was being said, so finally I interrupted by clearing my throat.

"Greetings, friend Matthew!" The Apostle and the angel both turned and smiled. "Glad you could make it, Todd. This place is beautiful scenery."

"Yes, I've been here before. Great place for taking pictures."

I pulled out my Nikon and motioned to Matthew and Calia.

"Mind if I snap a quick one? For memories?"

The Apostle looked at Calia. She smiled and stepped over to where I was.

"Todd," she said not unkindly, "My normal response would be to tell you no." She grinned a bit, then. "But I think, instead, I will tell you that there's no film in your camera."

I quickly checked the cartridge and realized she was right. When I had polished off the fourth roll in my rusty lug nuts adventure, I had uncharacteristically neglected to refill the camera. And I had none extra with me, which was especially unlike me.

"C'mon," Calia continued. "Matthew's been looking forward to seeing you. Let's walk."

"Well, friend Todd, I guess your sketches will have to do, at least for now," Matthew smiled and clapped me on the shoulder, then shook my hand in formal greeting.

"I guess so ..."

I don't know if it was because I couldn't take pictures or because it really was so, but almost immediately light began framing itself around structures at the arboretum. We walked past a bubbling pond and I had to stifle the reflex to pull out the camera. A stream with a garland of wildflowers at its edge simply made me clench my teeth. And in the fruit orchard, a single apple dangling from a limb just begged to be photographed. But in the end I walked on by, chatting with Matthew, enjoying the scenery, and secretly trying to memorize Calia's features so I could draw them later that night in my sketchpad.

We strolled around the grounds for at least an hour before deciding to sit and relax in the children's garden for a while. After a moment, we all fell silent, and I realized that, like my miraculous mentor here, I was becoming much more comfortable with the absence of words in a conversation.

It was in the stillness that the enormity of what I was experiencing finally began to sink in. I, Todd Striker, was sitting in a garden next to a man who'd been dead for thousands of years and next to a woman who by all appearances was an *actual* angel of God. And the man beside me, breathing in and out as though he'd never been forced to stop? He was not just any old Joe, but one who had helped change the course of history, one who had actually seen and heard and touched the Son of God.

And now he was here, and his sole purpose was simply to talk to *me*.

It was ludicrous. It seemed unreal, like some Hollywood fairy tale or ancient fable. Yet here I sat, and everything within me, every one of my senses, told me this was truly happening; that it was real, as real as my own hand that now patted the ground in nervous anticipation.

"So, Todd," Matthew broke the silence. "What is your question for today?"

I looked over at my friend, and realized just how old he was beginning to look. Oh, he hadn't aged, really. Not since I first met him back at the beginning of summer. But in his eyes there had been a graying of sorts, a weariness that was imperceptible at first but which now seemed to refuse to hide behind the twinkle that also dwelt there.

"I do have a question, Matthew. An important one. And it has to do with you."

"What is it?"

"Why would God send you here, Matthew? Just to answer my questions? That seems a little extreme. Why not just send a pastor over, or some Christian leader around town. Why would God go to this much trouble, Matthew? To transfer you from eternity and smack dab into my world? Just because I was mad at Him? Because I had questions? Why would God do this? Just for me?"

"I believe you already know the answer to that question, Todd."

I nodded. I had hoped I knew the answer, but it also led me to the more serious query. The one to which I wasn't so sure of the answer.

"I guess you're right, Matthew. The answer is obvious. So I suppose my real question, then, is this: can Jesus truly love me *that much?* To go to such lengths just so I will learn to know him?"

Matthew didn't respond at first. Then he said, "I'll tell you the truth, Todd, and it is a truth I hope you will never, ever release from your mind and heart.

"Jesus will go to any and all lengths to bring you to him. To restore what was stolen from all of us back when the serpent tread in the Garden of Eden. In fact, he already has."

"What do you mean?"

Matthew sat back and gave me a rueful smile. "It's a day I don't like to remember, but also one that must never be forgotten, because it was on that day that Christ gave his all, just for you. Just for me. Just for anyone who would dare to come to him. It was on that day that Jesus proved he loved us all ... *that much.*"

"Tell me, Matthew. Tell me the story one more time. I need to hear it."

He nodded, pausing a moment to collect his memories and put them in proper order. Then he leaned forward, assuming the storyteller role I'd seen from him just a few times before. "It begins," he said, "with a terrible, wonderful, bloody night of prayer ..."

Jesus went with his disciples to a place called Gethsemane, and he said to them, "Sit here while I go over there and pray." He took Peter and the two sons of Zebedee along with him, and he began to be sorrowful and troubled. Then he said to them, "My soul is overwhelmed with sorrow to the point of death. Stay here and keep watch with me."

Going a little farther, he fell with his face to the ground and prayed, "My Father, if it is possible, may this cup be taken from me. Yet not as I will, but as you will." Then he returned to his disciples and found them sleeping.

"Could you men not keep watch with me for one hour?" he asked Peter. "Watch and pray so that you will not fall into temptation. The spirit is willing, but the body is weak."

He went away a second time and prayed, "My Father, if it is not possible for this cup to be taken away unless I drink it, may your will be done."

When he came back, he again found them sleeping, because their eyes were heavy. So he left them and went away once more and prayed the third time, saying the same thing.

Then he returned to the disciples and said to them, "Are you still sleeping and resting? Look, the hour is near, and the Son of Man is betrayed into the hands of sinners. Rise, let us go! He re comes my betrayer!"

While he was still speaking, Judas, one of the Twelve, arrived. With him was a large crowd armed with swords and clubs, sent from the chief priests and the elders of the people.

Matthew closed his eyes, then—reliving the images of the night. I saw his face crinkle into a mask of regret and sorrowful anticipation. But he did not stop the story, and I clung to each word as it fell from his lips ...

Now the betrayer had arranged a signal with them: "The one I kiss is the man; arrest him." Going at once to Jesus, Judas said, "Greetings, Rabbi!"
And he kissed him.
Jesus replied, "Friend, do what you came for."
Then the men stepped forward, seized Jesus and arrested him. With that, one of Jesus' companions reached for his sword, drew it out and struck the servant of the high priest, cutting off his ear.
"Put your sword back in its place," Jesus said to him, "for all who draw the sword will die by the sword.
"Do you think I cannot call on my Father, and he will at once put at my disposal more than twelve legions of angels? But how then would the Scriptures be fulfilled that say it must happen in this way?"

"So, he could have skipped this whole episode?" I interrupted. "Is that what you're saying? He could have walked away, untouched, from what was about to come? And he refused?"
Matthew didn't open his eyes, but he nodded, a short, quick gesture that affirmed the answer to my question. Jesus didn't have to die, it seemed to say. But he did it anyway. For you. And for me.
The Apostle took a deep breath, and continued ...

At that time Jesus said to the crowd, "Am I leading a

rebellion, that you have come out with swords and clubs to capture me? Every day I sat in the temple courts teaching, and you did not arrest me. But this has all taken place that the writings of the prophets might be fulfilled."

Then, *all* the disciples deserted him and fled.

Those who had arrested Jesus took him to Caiaphas, the high priest, where the teachers of the law and the elders had assembled. But Peter followed him at a distance, right up to the courtyard of the high priest. He entered and sat down with the guards to see the outcome.

The chief priests and the whole Sanhedrin were looking for false evidence against Jesus so that they could put him to death. But they did not find any, though many false witnesses came forward.

Finally two came forward and declared, "This fellow said, 'I am able to destroy the temple of God and rebuild it in three days.'"

Then the high priest stood up and said to Jesus, "Are you not going to answer? What is this testimony that these men are bringing against you?" But Jesus remained silent.

The high priest said to him, "I charge you under oath by the living God: Tell us if you are the Christ, the Son of God."

"Yes, it is as you say," Jesus replied. "But I say to all of you: In the future you will see the Son of Man sitting at the right hand of the Mighty One and coming on the clouds of heaven."

Then the high priest tore his clothes and said, "He has spoken blasphemy! Why do we need any more witnesses? Look, now you have heard the blasphemy. What do you think?"

"He is worthy of death," they answered

Then they spit in his face and struck him with their fists. Others slapped him and said, "Prophesy to us, Christ. Who hit you?"

Early in the morning, all the chief priests and the elders of the people came to the decision to put Jesus to death. They bound him, led him away, and handed him over to Pilate, the governor.

When Judas, who had betrayed him, saw that Jesus was condemned, he was seized with remorse and returned the thirty silver coins to the chief priests and the elders.

"I have sinned," he said, "for I have betrayed innocent blood."

"What is that to us?" they replied. "That's your responsibility."

So Judas threw the money into the temple and left. Then he went away and hanged himself.

The chief priests picked up the coins and said, "It is against the law to put this into the treasury, since it is blood money." So they decided to use the money to buy the potter's field as a burial place for foreigners. That is why it has been called the Field of Blood to this day. Then what was spoken by Jeremiah the prophet was fulfilled: "They took the thirty silver coins, the price set on him by the people of Israel, and they used them to buy the potter's field, as the Lord commanded me."

Meanwhile Jesus stood before the governor, and the governor asked him, "Are you the king of the Jews?"

"Yes, it is as you say," Jesus replied.

When he was accused by the chief priests and the elders, he gave no answer. Then Pilate asked him, "Don't you hear the testimony they are bringing against you?"

But Jesus made no reply, not even to a single charge—to the great amazement of the governor.

Now it was the governor's custom at the Feast to release a prisoner chosen by the crowd. At that time they had a notorious prisoner, called Barabbas. So when the crowd had gathered, Pilate asked them, "Which one do you want me to release to you: Barabbas, or Jesus who is called Christ?" For he knew it was out of envy that they had handed Jesus over to him.

While Pilate was sitting on the judge's seat, his wife sent him this message: "Don't have anything to do with that innocent man, for I have suffered a great deal today in a dream because of him."

But the chief priests and the elders persuaded the crowd to ask for Barabbas and to have Jesus executed.

"Which of the two do you want me to release to you?" asked the governor.

"Barabbas," they answered.

"What shall I do, then, with Jesus who is called Christ?" Pilate asked.

They all answered, "Crucify him!"

"Why? What crime has he committed?" asked Pilate.

But they shouted all the louder, "Crucify him!"

When Pilate saw that he was getting nowhere, but that instead an uproar was starting, he took water and washed his hands in front of the crowd. "I am innocent of this man's blood," he said. "It is your responsibility!"

All the people answered, "Let his blood be on us and on our children!"

Then he released Barabbas to them.

But he had Jesus flogged, and handed him over to be crucified.

Then the governor's soldiers took Jesus into the Praetorium and gathered the whole company of soldiers around him. They stripped him and put a scarlet robe on him, and then twisted together a crown of thorns and set it on his head. They put a staff in his right hand and knelt in front of him and mocked him.

"Hail, king of the Jews!" they said. They spit on him, and took the staff and struck him on the head again and again. After they had mocked him, they took off the robe and put his own clothes on him. Then they led him away to crucify him.

As they were going out, they met a man from Cyrene, named Simon, and they forced him to carry the cross. They came to a place called Golgotha (which means The Place of the Skull). There they offered Jesus wine to drink, mixed with gall; but after tasting it, he refused to drink it.

When they had crucified him, they divided up his clothes by casting lots. And sitting down, they kept watch over him there. Above his head they placed the written charge against him: THIS IS JESUS, THE KING OF THE JEWS.

Two robbers were crucified with him, one on his right and one on his left. Those who passed by hurled insults at him, shaking their heads and saying, "You who are going to destroy the temple and build it in three days, save yourself! Come down from the cross, if you are the Son of God!"

In the same way the chief priests, the teachers of the law and the elders mocked him.

"He saved others," they said, "but he can't save himself! He's the King of Israel! Let him come down now from the cross, and we will believe in him. He trusts in God. Let God rescue him now if he wants him, for he said, 'I am the Son of God.'" In the same way the robbers who were crucified with him also heaped insults on him.

From the sixth hour until the ninth hour darkness came over all the land. About the ninth hour Jesus cried out in a loud voice, *"Eloi, Eloi,* lama *sabachthani?"*—which means, "My God, my God, why have you forsaken me?"

When some of those standing there heard this, they said, "He's calling Elijah." Immediately one of them ran and got a sponge. He filled it with wine vinegar, put it on a stick, and offered it to Jesus to drink. The rest said, "Now leave him alone. Let's see if Elijah comes to save him."

And when Jesus had cried out again in a loud voice, he

gave up his spirit.

At that moment the curtain of the temple was torn in two from top to bottom.

The earth shook and the rocks split.

The tombs broke open and the bodies of many holy people who had died were raised to life. They came out of the tombs, and after Jesus' resurrection they went into the holy city and appeared to many people.

When the centurion and those with him who were guarding Jesus saw the earthquake and all that had happened, they were terrified, and exclaimed, "Surely he was the Son of God ..."

Matthew opened his eyes, then, and leaned back a bit. He looked exhausted, like a man who has cried so deeply for so long that the bitter, salty tears will no longer come.

"That, friend Todd," he said, "is how much Jesus loves you. Enough to endure the torture and agony of the cross. More so, enough to take upon himself all sin and sorrow—all responsibility for all evils. For you."

I nodded. The waves of understanding were finally beginning to break through the walls my heart had built up and fortified over so many years. That God might send Matthew to come answer my questions was no big thing, really. That he would send his son Jesus Christ to willingly die at the hands of murderous men, that he would allow Christ's blood to stain the dirty wood and darkened earth amidst the jeers of criminals and vengeful hypocrites, this was the true miracle. That he, an absolute innocent, would take up the punishment for my failures. This was true love.

"Matthew," I said finally, "I need this kind of love. Desperately."

"I know you do, Todd. And you can have it. Today. Right now."

And so I took it, there in the children's garden at the Fullerton Arboretum.

And I have never been the same.

...

It is late. Or early, depending on your perspective. I sit alone outside my little dome tent, wrapped up in flannel and thick socks, with my sleeping bag pulled in tightly over my body.

It is cold. And dark. Were it brighter, I know I would be able to see my breath as it expels from my nostrils. I have a knit cap secured over my ears, yet they still feel the bite of the cold. I'm not sure how long I can endure the creeping chill that has begun to take over my extremities.

But they tell me it is worth it. They tell me to stick it out, and I will be glad I did.

So I sit, staring out over the night-blackened water of Lake Tahoe. Waiting.

I was curious that no other campers seemed even within shouting distance when I arrived. But it is December, and the cold has kept them away.

December is the best month, my so-called friends had told me. Nothing to interfere with the view. Quiet. Peace.

I feel like cursing those friends now. But instead, I wait.

Inside my sleeping bag, my gloved hands grip a camera. An expensive Canon, with superb zoom capability. I begin to wonder if I can operate it with my gloves off, or if my fingers will be too frozen to push the buttons and spin the zoom lens.

A crack appears in the darkness.

I take in a breath, involuntarily. I can now make out the dark blueness of the water that laps up on the shore nearby, finally matching the sound with the movement.

It won't be long now.

I am too scared to close my eyes. After all this time, I don't want to miss this. Another streak peeks over the horizon. Reddish-orange. Or is it yellow? I begin peeling off my warmth, allowing the sleeping bag to drop by my side. Stripping the gloves from my hands.

It has been so gradual up to this point, that the actual sunrise surprises me. One moment I am in darkness shadowed by streaks of light. The next, there is nothing but blistering, beautiful, color-drenched sky.

The morning has come.

At first I am so dazzled I forget why I am here. Then my instincts kick in and I begin flicking open and closed the shutter on my camera, doing my best to capture this moment on film.

Somewhere in between the first and second rolls, I finally understand what my friends had been telling me about for so long. And that they were right.

I am so glad I came!

• • •

The Twelfth Tuesday

We Talk about Life

THE FOLLOWING TUESDAY threatened to be an impossibly good day. For starters, I was very much looking forward to a lunch meeting with Matthew. After last week, I realized that not only had I found an answer to my questions, I had also opened a door to a new life filled with even more questions. I decided to start writing them down, making a list so to speak, so that I wouldn't forget to cover them with Matthew.

By Thursday night I had forty-one queries for the Apostle. I thought of numbers forty-two and forty-three while brushing my teeth Friday morning. After listening to the sermon on Sunday (yes, I went back to that church in Fullerton), I was up to fifty-eight. When I hit sixty, I forced myself to stop, at least for the time being. I figured that if Matthew and I could cover five question per Tuesday, that would be enough to match the amount time we'd spend together so far, and that was a good enough goal to start with.

A second bright spot of my day was the promise of dinner with Miranda. She had accepted my first invitation the previous week. We met for lunch after church on Sunday and ended up spending the whole afternoon together. When I called her on Monday to suggest a second date, she accepted. And now I was looking forward to picking her up after my time with Matthew ended for the day.

Add to that extremely pleasant weather, and the fact that I'd slept like a baby the night before, and this day was shaping up to rank at least as one of my top twenty so far. The cancellation of a photo assignment and even a small scratch on the door of my car couldn't even damper my mood.

I found that although my life was very much the same on the outside—same routines, same frustrations, same everything—there was a difference within me that was hard to describe. A peaceful Presence that seemed to remind me moment by moment that there is a God—and that he loves me. When I awoke with that thought in my head, I knew this Tuesday was going to be a special one, regardless of what might happen during the day.

Jackson was coming down the stairs as I walked up them on my way to apartment number 23 at the Breezewood Arms. He nodded his greeting to me, and I noticed a few errant streaks of white in his hair, with a nice little dollop of paint on the tip of his left ear. He carried a bucket with water and a few paintbrushes, apparently heading down to rinse them all out at that faucet by the laundry room.

"Been redecorating again?" I asked.

"Just a little," he said as he passed me on the steps. "Matthew is napping, so just walk on in without knocking up there. I already told Calia you were here."

The door to the apartment was unlocked, so I took Jackson's advice and walked in, careful not to slam the door behind me for fear of waking the Apostle. The first thing I noticed was the walls. Jackson had been at work, all right, and I have to say that for once the place was worse off for it.

Where there had once been that marvelous lumines-cent paint that seemed to change its radiance in relation to the sun, there now was a drab whiteness that mimicked the décor of thousands of cookie-cutter apartments in the area. He'd apparently covered over everything with tex-ture, then repainted the walls to reflect the more "normal" look you'd expect to see.

I was disappointed with the change in colors, but the furniture was all still the same, at least. Calia soon entered from the kitchen, and her presence alone seemed to brighten up the room as well.

"Hello, Todd," she smiled. "High noon it is, and you're right on time."

"Is he around?" I asked, accepting the tall glass of Mountain Dew she offered.

For the first time ever, I thought I saw a flicker of uncertainty in the eyes of my herald angel. But that mil-lisecond soon passed, and she said, "He's been resting for a while, but why don't you have a seat and I'll go check on him. I know he won't want to miss any time with you today."

The room smelled heavenly, like a mixture of lilac bushes and light perfume. I drank in the aroma as I sat down on the futon in the living room. After a few moments—longer than I expected, really—the door to the bedroom opened. Matthew looked a little tired around the eyes, but otherwise his fit, normal self. He even had man-aged to dress respectably this day, wearing what looked to be comfortable Levis jean shorts, a white T-shirt, and a dark blue, short-sleeved overshirt that was unbuttoned in the typical California style. His feet were bare, but on his head was that old familiar Disney cap I'd given him several weeks before.

"Greetings, friend Todd," he said warmly. I stood and shook his hand, then nodded toward his hat.

"'Bout time for me to find you a new one of those," I said. "That one seems to have gotten its share of the limelight."

He smiled and motioned for me to return to my seat, and he settled into the wingback chair beside me.

"It's good to see you again," he said.

"Thanks. Good to see you too."

There was a moment when nothing was said, and it took me two or three full minutes before I even noticed. I felt a warm, comfortable glow just sitting in his apartment, and conversation was only an added plus. Finally I pulled out my list of questions and laid them out before me.

"Been an interesting week for me," I said. "A good one."

The Apostle smiled. "I can imagine."

"And I've been busy, thinking about you and me. In fact, I've been jotting down a whole list of new questions for you."

He laughed. "Well," he said, "that is why I'm here. For now at least."

I started scanning down the questions, trying to choose just the right one for this day. All of a sudden, they all seemed to leave something to be desired. I flipped through the pages, searching for something that was appropriate, when his hand reached over and gently pushed the pages down onto the coffee table.

"Todd," he said, "there'll be plenty of time for these questions—and the hundreds more you will have in your lifetime—later. But for now, why don't you just ask me what you really want to ask."

I thought back over my passage through the past three months or so. Of the time I first met Calia and Jackson and of the days when I did all that I could to chase away the man they called the Apostle. I thought about the memories he had stirred up within me, and the questions I had hidden for so many years that he brought out into the light. I thought about how, just one short week ago, he had finally helped me to come into the light myself.

"Matthew," I said finally, "I guess the most important question I have today is, what now?"

"What now?" he repeated, as if saying the words again would be the start of the answer.

"Yes. I feel as though I have been on a long walk through a darkened tunnel. Last week I finally reached the end of the tunnel and stepped into the warmth and light of the sunshine. And as I stand blinking in the light, I can't help but think this is not the end of my journey. That it's really, at long last, only just the beginning. And the question that comes to mind then, is: what now?"

The Apostle nodded and looked thoughtfully into my face. "I asked that question once, under circumstances that were both similar and different."

"What was the answer?"

"Well, let's see. It was on a Friday. That terrible, wonderful Friday when I first asked it of God. My heart cried those words to him when death crept from the pits of hell and stole away my master, Jesus Christ. It kept crying out, unanswered, through the hours that passed on Saturday. I went to sleep with no response. Then Sunday morning, I was surprised by life.

"And that, friend Todd, was my answer."

"I don't think I know what you mean, Matthew."

"Death took Jesus from us, Todd," he said. "And it was necessary. Christ alone could pay that death penalty for you and me. But that was not enough. It could never hold him for long.

"He surprised death, astonished eternity, by walking out of the grave on that world-changing Sunday morning. He shocked even those of us who were his disciples, if the truth were known. And when he came back to life, he brought back with him Life—with a capital 'L.'

"It was the women who found out first. I always thought there was a bit of divine irony in that. I mean, those of us who called ourselves his disciples were nowhere to be found that Sunday morning. Truth is, we were all in hiding, scared out of our wits that the Romans and the Jewish religious leaders were now hunting for us. The cross is a terrible way to die, and at that time at least, none of us wanted to suffer it like Jesus did.

"But Mary Magdalene and another Mary couldn't be kept away. Dead or alive, he was still her Lord and Master. So she went to the tomb.

"They found an earthquake!"

Matthew stole an approving glance at Calia, then continued. "An angel of God came down from heaven and made the earth shake beneath them. He walked right up to the large stone that covered the entrance to Christ's grave, then tossed it aside like a pebble.

"Oh, what joy that angel must have felt! He propped himself up on that worthless old stone and told the women, 'I know that you are looking for Jesus, who was crucified ...'"

Matthew sucked in his breath, his eyes blazing with excitement, *"'He is not here. He* has risen, just as he said ...'

"Oh that I could have been there to hear the angel speak those words! But I found out from Mary soon after, and that was enough. He was alive. That was the glorious surprise he brought to me. To all of us. The surprise of Life.

"So you ask me, 'what now?' And I say to you the answer is this: Now—and only now—you can experience the awesome, life-altering surprise of true, eternal, unimaginable Life."

"But how?"

"Don't you see, Todd? Jesus is no longer dead. He is alive, right now, this very second. He holds the power of

Life in his hands …"

"And he holds me in his heart … Yes, Matthew, I am just beginning to see."

"Life is in him, Todd. Each day that you spend growing closer to Jesus, you spend discovering a brand new surprise about Life. And that, my friend is a joyful task that will last you forever and beyond." He cocked his head to one side, then, and smiled. "Trust me on this one, Todd. I know it from experience."

"Life. Growth. Eternity. I feel like a baby again, only this time I get to skip the diapers and strained carrots."

He laughed, and in the back of my mind I hoped that I would always be able to remember that laugh. A hearty, uninhibited expression that seemed to see more than the lame joke I'd just cracked. I grinned. It was nice to think an Apostle would laugh at your feeble attempts at humor.

After a moment, his chuckles subsided into a sigh. "It will be nice to spend forever with you, Todd."

"I think that's the best compliment I've ever received, Matthew."

He didn't say anything, just reached out to pat me gently on the shoulder. It reminded me of my father. The crinkles at the corner of his eyes seemed to deepen just then, and Calia unexpectedly stood up between us. Matthew nodded to her briefly, but then turned back his attention to me.

"I've enjoyed spending time with you, Todd. Very much. Your father was right about you."

"I've had a good day with you too, Matthew."

"I am sorry to say that all these weeks here are beginning to catch up to me. I'm not the young man I once was, you know!"

"Of course. I'm sorry. You should rest. We can talk more again next Tuesday."

"Rest sounds very good to me right now, Todd."

I took a cue from Calia and stood up too. The Apostle stood next to me. He did look so very tired.

"Matthew," I said. "Thank you for coming. Thank you for everything. You've changed my life, and I'm grateful."

He waved off my comment. "I didn't change your life, Todd. I was simply a part of your life. It's Jesus who's been changing it. And I must tell you, my friend, he's just getting started!"

"I'm looking forward to getting to know him better," I said. "To being surprised by his Life in me."

The Apostle placed one hand on each of my shoulders, and before I could react, gave me a quick kiss on each cheek. "I know this isn't done in your society anymore," he said. "But where I come from, it was done among close friends. And I consider you a very close friend, Todd."

"Thanks, Matthew."

Calia spoke something to Matthew in Aramaic, then, and he nodded in agreement.

"Shalom! Peace, friend Todd. May God's peace rest on you always."

"You too, Matthew. See you next Tuesday?"

The Apostle didn't respond, and instead turned his weary form toward the bedroom. Calia walked him to the bedroom door, then gently shut it behind him.

"Is it time?" Jackson now stood in the front entrance, looking back toward the bedroom. A sudden fear gripped my heart, as though I had missed the obvious and now it might be too late.

"Almost," Calia replied. "You OK, Todd?"

"I—I think so," I said nervously.

Jackson walked to where I was and extended his hand. "It's been a pleasure, Todd."

I shook, my mind racing.

"Yes, Todd," Calia spoke next. "I will always treasure this time."

"Wait a minute," I said. "You guys are acting like this is goodbye. I'll see you next week, right? Right?"

Neither angel said anything. An adrenaline-fueled feeling of near panic flooded through me. Without stopping to ask permission, I bolted toward the bedroom door and rushed in to see Matthew. I expected to find him resting comfortably in a bed. At least I hoped to find that.

But the room was empty.

The walls were the same drab color as the newly painted living room. The carpet was brown, old, and flat. The window was curtainless, closed, and locked shut. There was nothing else there. Nothing.

I stumbled to the closet door and flung it open. Inside, hanging on a hook, was a slightly beat-up, lovingly-worn baseball cap featuring the smiling faces of Mickey Mouse, Donald Duck, and Goofy. It is all that I have left of him. That and my sketches.

I cannot describe the feeling of loss I felt at that moment. The sadness came near to that which gripped me when my father left this world. But, unsuspectedly, this time it was soon replaced by an unusual joy.

"I will see you again, Matthew," I whispered. "You can count on it."

When I returned to the living room, I was only partly surprised to find it empty as well. My angels were nowhere in sight, and apparently they'd taken all the furniture with them when they left. The bare little apartment now even had vacuumed floors. It's amazing what angels can do when they set their minds to it.

At first I secretly hoped that I would see at least them again. But then I remembered Calia's words at one of our earliest meetings: "If we don't want you to find us, you won't. If we do want you to find us, you will. That's just kind of the way things work, you know?"

I have never seen my angels since, though I have often suspected the faithful Jackson was nearby, especially at moments of almost-tragedy that happen near me or someone I love.

I stood in the empty little rooms of number 23 at 12222 Breezewood for just a while longer on that last Tuesday in September. I will be honest. A few tears did flow.

Finally I looked toward the ceiling and spoke, "Well, Jesus. Looks like it's just you and me now."

And deep within my spirit, I knew that would be enough.

Epilogue

IT'S BEEN TWO DECADES since I've looked at one, and now I feel my hands tremble slightly. Silly, I think, to be nervous about something like this. But nervous I am.

I don't know why, but when the sales clerk asked me what kind of Bible I wanted, I asked for a kids' version.

"Stories? Or full text?" she asked pleasantly.

"Um, full text I think."

I never knew there were so many to choose from!

So now I sit in my own little condominium opening the spine of a Bible, one that's been translated into language a child can understand and, much to my delight, is filled with pictures.

Matthew is gone, yet I still have so many questions. But for the first time in my life, I believe that's OK. I don't need to know all the answers. That's God's job, I guess. But I do need someone to help me tackle the questions like Matthew did. I figure that's also God's job, and that maybe it's time for me to take advantage of one of the major tools he's given to help me understand.

So I open to the New Testament. I will start here, at the beginning. At the place where my new life began seventeen months ago.

"The book of the genealogy of Jesus Christ," it reads, "the Son of David, the son of Abraham ..."

As I scan the pages, I can't help but picture a short, balding man, hunched over a parchment and scratching out these words that will, over time, be read by billions. And, as the sentences begin flowing into my hungry spirit, I imagine that man is clapping my father on the back. And both of them are smiling.

Scripture References

The First Tuesday: ....Matthew 1:18-25 (Jesus' birth)

The Second Tuesday:.................................Matthew 4:1-11
   (Jesus' Temptation in Wilderness)

The Third Tuesday: ....Matthew 6:5-13
   (The Lord's Prayer)

The Fourth Tuesday: ....Matthew 9:9-13
   (The Call of Matthew)

The Fifth Tuesday: ....Matthew 13:24-30; 36-43
   (Parable of the Wheat & Weeds)

The Sixth Tuesday: ....Matthew 13:45-46; 19:16-30
   (Parable of the Pearl of Great Price; Story of the Rich
   Young Ruler)

The Seventh Tuesday: ....Matthew 19:13-15
   (Children & the Kingdom)

The Eighth Tuesday: ....Matthew 20:20-28
   (Greatest in the Kingdom)

The Ninth Tuesday: ....Matthew 21:1-11
   (The Triumphal Entry)

The Tenth Tuesday: ....Matthew 26:31-35; 26:57-27:31
   (Peter's Denial)

The Eleventh Tuesday: ....Matthew 26:36-68, 27:1-54
   (Jesus' Crucifixion)

The Twelfth Tuesday: ....Matthew 28:1-10
   (Jesus' Resurrection)

Acknowledgments

I am indebted to a great many people for this book. First to my editor, Craig Bubeck, who caught the vision behind a "Christian Living Novel" and was willing to risk his reputation alongside mine in order to make it available to the public.

To my friends, Robin Jones Gunn, Jefferson Scott, and Dr. Norm Wakefield, who so graciously endorsed this manuscript (and also risked their reputations on my behalf!).

To my pastor, Kent Hummel, who constantly challenges me to go deeper, live stronger, and to seek the face of Christ.

To the following reference works that lent valuable background information during my research for this book: *The Holy Bible, English Standard Version* (Crossway Books, 2001); *The Holy Bible, New International Version* (Zondervan, 1984); *The Holy Bible, New Living Translation* (Tyndale House Publishers, 1996); *The Quest Study Bible* (Zondervan, 1994), *The New Manners and Customs of Bible Times* by Ralph Gower (Moody Press, 1987); *The IVP Bible Background Commentary: New Testament* by Craig S. Keener (InterVarsity Press, 1993); *Daily Life at the Time of Jesus* by Miriam Feinberg Vamosh (Concordia Publishing House, no publication date given); *The New Testament Explorer* by Mark Bailey & Tom Constable (Word Publishing, 1999); *The Illustrated Life of Jesus* by Herschel Hobbs (Holman Publishers, 2000); *Willmington's Bible Handbook* by Harold L. Willmington (Tyndale, 1997); and *Who Was Who in the Bible* (Thomas Nelson Publishers, 1999).

To the apostle Matthew who lived an inspiring life and left behind a legacy that has literally revolutionized the world many times over.

And last—but most assuredly not least—to Jesus Christ, who is never afraid of my questions and who gives me the only reason I have to write.

If you enjoyed "Tuesdays with Matthew" you're sure to also enjoy "Who Moved My Church?" by Mike Nappa!

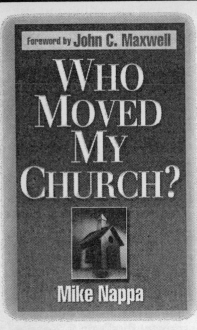

Who Moved My Church?
Mike Nappa

How would people respond if they showed up at church one Sunday morning only to discover someone or something had actually, physically moved it?

Undoubtedly, they would go out and find it! And that's what four unforgettable characters from *Who Moved My Church?* set out to do!

Nappa's parable will spur church attendees to tackle one of the enduring questions of Christian history: How is the Church to interact with culture? The question is all the more pressing for pastors and laity in light of dramatic and rapid changes taking place in society on what feels like a daily basis.

Humorous, entertaining, and thought provoking, *Who Moved My Church?* will be the center of discussion in homes, small groups, Sunday school classes and churches everywhere.

ISBN: 1-58919-990-1   **ITEM #:** RO-990
Format: Hardcover   Size: 5-1/2 x 8-1/2
Pages: 128

"Mike Nappa has written an intelligent, clever, and explosive book that challenges the people of God to consider what kind of influence they will wield in the world today. You will laugh, cry, probably get mad, and most importantly, think."

—*John C. Maxwell*

Order your copies today!
Order online: www.cookministries.com
Phone: 1-800-323-7543
Or visit your local Christian bookstore.

More Great Fiction from Cook— *The Award-Winning American Family Portrait Series*

by Jack Cavanaugh

Travel through American history and follow the legacy of Christian faith being passed from generation to generation in the Morgan family.

Format: Paperback   Size: 5-7/16 x 8-1/2

The Puritans—Book #1
Drew Morgan, a young Englishman, dreams of being a knight, but finds love and faith in the New World.
ISBN: 1-56476-440-0   **ITEM #:** 59550
Pages: 432

The Colonists—Book #2
From the cobbled streets of Boston to a Narragansett Indian village to the Atlantic's high seas. Could the family's Christian heritage be in jeopardy?
ISBN: 1-56476-346-3   **ITEM #:** 59568
Pages: 486

The Patriots—Book #3
The lifelong rivalry of Esau and Jacob Morgan reaches its pinnacle during the American War for independence.
ISBN: 1-56476-428-1   **ITEM #:** 59576
Pages: 500

The Adversaries—Book #4
As the Civil War erupts, the children of Jeremiah Morgan are uprooted from home—the boys to the battlefields, their only sister to New York City. Their greatest peril, however, may come from banker Caleb McKenna, a longtime family enemy.
ISBN: 1-56476-535-0   **ITEM #:** 59584
Pages: 552

Order Your Copies Today!
Order Online: www.cookministries.com
Phone: 1-800-323-7543
Or Visit your Local Christian Bookstore

More of *The Award-Winning American Family Portrait Series*
by Jack Cavanaugh

The Pioneers—Book #5
Fleeing crime and corruption in New York, Jesse Morgan heads for the plains of the exciting Midwest, but Jesse isn't just running from the city—he's running from God.
ISBN: 1-56476-587-3   **ITEM #:** 59592
Pages: 432

The Allies—Book #6
World War I impacts the Morgan family as Katherine serves as a nurse, while her brother Johnnie becomes a pilot in the American Expeditionary Forces.
ISBN: 1-56476-588-1   **ITEM #:** 59600
Pages: 475

The Victors—Book #7
Four siblings are caught up in the events of World War II. Nat, Walt, Alex, and Lily Morgan will each face life's worst before they find out what it really means to be "the victors."
ISBN: 1-56476-589-X   **ITEM #:** 59618
Pages: 500

The Peacemakers—Book #8
How will the 13th generation of Morgans tackle the challenges of the 1960's, the Vietnam War, social protest, and assassinations?
ISBN: 1-56476-681-0   **ITEM #:** 63743
Pages: 512

Order Your Copies Today!
Order Online: www.cookministries.com
Phone: 1-800-323-7543
Or Visit your Local Christian Bookstore

Good News in fiction!
Enjoy these three books by Gary E. Parker

The Last Gift
A Christmas Story about Family Forgiveness

It's Christmas Eve, and 40-year-old Christina returns to her childhood home for the annual family reunion. However, the joys of the holidays escape her. *The Last Gift* focuses on the importance of family forgiveness and centers around a missing locket, the heirloom of the women in the family.

ISBN: 1-56476-779-5 **ITEM #:** 64931
Format: Hardcover Size: 5 x 7
Pages: 112 Brand: Victor

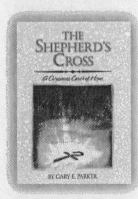

The Shepherd's Cross
A Christmas Carol of Hope

Christmas Eve is the wrong time to be laid off, especially with a wife, two kids, and another on the way. Discover how three mysterious encounters the night before Christmas help start Chipper on a journey to healing—for himself and his family.

ISBN: 0-78143-694-X **ITEM #:** 100727
Format: Hardcover Size: 5 x 7
Pages: 144 Brand: Victor

The Wedding Dress

Thirty-one-year-old Rachel Lewis learns a family secret when her Alzheimer's-stricken mom suddenly becomes lucid one rainy Mother's Day afternoon. What Rachel decides to do with this new information will not only change her own life but the lives of those around her.

ISBN: 0-78143-700-8 **ITEM #:** 100772
Format: Hardcover Size: 5 x 7
Pages: 112 Brand: Victor

Order your copies today!
Order online: www.cookministries.com
Phone: 1-800-323-7543
Or visit your local Christian bookstore.

An Apocolyptic Thriller
from Joseph Bayly

Winterflight

Set in the not-so-distant future, this chilling tale challenges readers to consider how America's apathy and inaction may soon lead to a society of legal terminations and genetically perfected populations. Inspires Christians to respond to the issues of their day with conviction, courage, and truth.

ISBN: 1-56476-786-8   ITEM #: 71464
Format: Paperback
Size: 5-1/2 x 8-1/2
Pages: 180

Order your copies today!
Order online: www.cookministries.com
Phone: 1-800-323-7543
Or visit your local Christian bookstore.